The Last Tales of Uncle Remus

The Tales of Uncle Remus
The Adventures of Brer Rabbit

More Tales of Uncle Remus
Further Adventures of Brer Rabbit,
His Friends, Enemies, and Others

Further Tales of Uncle Remus
The Misadventures of Brer Rabbit,
Brer Fox, Brer Wolf, the Doodang,
and Other Creatures

The Last Tales of Uncle Remus

•

Long Journey Home
Stories from Black History

This Strange New Feeling

The Knee-High Man *And Other Tales*

To Be a Slave

The Last Tales of Uncle Remus

as told by JULIUS LESTER

illustrated by Jerry Pinkney

D I A L B O O K S

New York

Published by Dial Books
A Division of Penguin Books USA Inc.
375 Hudson Street
New York, New York 10014
Text copyright © 1994 by Julius Lester
Pictures copyright © 1994 by Jerry Pinkney
All rights reserved
Design by Jane Byers Bierhorst
Printed in the U.S.A.
First Edition
10 9 8 7 6 5 4 3

Library of Congress Cataloging in Publication Data

Lester, Julius.
The last tales of Uncle Remus : as told by Julius Lester
illustrated by Jerry Pinkney.—1st ed.
p.   cm.
Summary : Retells the final adventures and misadventures
of Brer Rabbit and his friends and enemies.
ISBN 0-8037-1303-7.—ISBN 0-8037-1304-5 (lib. bdg.)
1. Afro-Americans—Folklore. 2. Tales—United States.
[1. Folklore, Afro-American. 2. Animals—Folklore.]
I. Pinkney, Jerry, ill. II. Title.
PZ8.1.L434Las   1994
398.2'08996073—dc20   93-7531   CIP   AC

The publisher wishes to express its sincere thanks to the estate
of Joel Chandler Harris for its gracious support during the
publication of this new version of *The Tales of Uncle Remus*.

*Each black-and-white drawing is made of pencil and graphite; and
each full-color picture consists of a pencil, graphite, and watercolor
painting that is color-separated and reproduced in full color.*

To Phyllis Fogelman
J. L.

To the memory of my father,
James H., and to Julius Lester
J. P.

Since the first volume of my retelling of *The Tales of Uncle Remus* appeared in 1987, a question I have been asked often is, "Why did you keep the name of Uncle Remus?"

Behind the question I hear a concern that by retaining the name, I may have also retained the unpleasant historical memories evoked by a name of plantation slavery. My response has been that the title, *The Tales of Uncle Remus,* identifies a particular collection of Afro-American folktales, the largest single body we have.

However, as I completed work on this, the fourth and last volume, I began wondering why *The Tales of Uncle Remus* have endured in people's affections to an extent far greater than anything else in American folklore. Since 1987 I have met many people who grew up being read *The Tales of Uncle Remus*. I have seen their bodies relax into childhood as they share memories of the experience of being read to by a mother or father.

The expressions of awe and wonder on their faces indicate that the memories evoked include more than the stories themselves, especially because often they do not recall particular stories, though they do remember Brer Rabbit. The memories are of a total experience, encompassing the tale, the setting in which the tale was heard, and the storyteller, the one in the flesh—parent, relative, teacher—and the one on the page, Uncle Remus. The experience evoked by the memories is of a relationship, a relationship for which the adult still yearns.

It is this relationship that is absent from many of the stories that appear in print today. As the function of storytelling has been taken over more and more by books, the voice of storytelling has become a disembodied one. The story has become words on pages supported and vivified by illustrations.

But storytelling is a human event, an act of creating relationship. In a traditional setting, storytelling creates and re–creates community, making a bond between the living and the living, the young and the old, the living and the dead, the human and the animal, the human and the vegetable and the mineral. The storyteller resides at the vortex of mystery, resolving it by means that do not rob us of mystery.

The genius of Joel Chandler Harris was creating Uncle Remus. It is difficult to separate the tales from the figure of Uncle

Remus. Quite rightly, Harris made story and storyteller one. If he had simply published the tales without the distinctive voice of the narrator, the stories would not have endured. It is Uncle Remus's belief in their veracity that enables us to suspend our rationality and be blessed by the magical act of the story.

Uncle Remus is more, however. He is the archetypal good father. He jokes, he teases, he pretends to be annoyed, he feigns anger and hurt when offended. But we know the truth of the man is his dignity, his self-respect, and above all, his love.

It is a love that is difficult to describe, especially in a time when love is sentimentalized in an unceasing effluvium of popular music, television dramas, and films. Thus, we forget or never learn that love is tough, that love has the brilliant hardness of diamonds, the cutting clarity of the most rational thought.

Uncle Remus loves tradition. For him tradition is not an act of preserving the past, but an understanding of values, values that a newer age has increasingly little sense of. Uncle Remus knows what is right and what is wrong and suffers no confusion or doubt about which is which. This is part of the comfort and safety generations of children have found in him and his storytelling. He represents certainty; and childhood, with its constant change and growth, is anything but secure and safe.

Uncle Remus also loves language. The language of storytelling is supposed to be a specialized one of startling images, absurd words, and amusing paradox. It is the language that gives these tales their special aliveness because the language startles us from the complacency of the ordinary into the vibrancy of the extraordinary. The language is so convincing, however, that we are not left in the world of fantasy but are returned to the ordinary where we find ourselves wanting to address a rabbit on the lawn as "Brer" and feeling disappointed that it won't answer.

Of course, I am aware that Harris's Uncle Remus also represents a slave plantation type—the servile "darky," loyal to white people, disparaging of other blacks, the privileged faithful servant who identifies with his oppressor and condition of oppression. As I pointed out in the introduction to the first volume of this series, I do not quarrel with history. Such blacks existed during slavery. Those who would criticize Uncle Remus for his accommodationist politics overlook the fact that it is the same Uncle Remus who preserved the culture through the tales. Without the Uncle Remuses, how much of black folk culture would have survived?

I note that Harris's Uncle Remus was in many respects an Uncle Tom. This should not blind us to his contribution or cause us to withdraw respect from him. Each of us is as complex and contradictory, and that is the beauty of being human.

So as I conclude this retelling, I understand that I retained the name of Uncle Remus and created my own version of him because the storyteller is as important as the story, if not more so. I wonder if generations have not read these tales as much for the tale-teller as for the tales themselves. And is this not logical? Do not our souls hunger for genuine experiences of others? Are not our spirits revived through contact with others whose spirits touch our spirits in a way that makes us feel better for having sat with them for a while? Is not the essence of our lives the desire to live in relationships that will return to us an image of ourselves that we can love?

This is the function of the storyteller and his or her story— to wed us with ourselves by wedding us to the mysteries that will always be, and at the same time animate us with laughter and love.

While a book may have a single author, the final product is a collaborative effort. I want to thank Jerry Pinkney for his wonderful illustrations in these four volumes. His work has enhanced the wonder of the tales, enriched their spirit, and complemented the language to create a whole bigger than the words could have alone.

Phyllis Fogelman, the editor-in-chief and publisher of Dial Books for Young Readers, and I have worked together for almost twenty-five years now. Since the publication of *To Be a Slave,* she has been the midwife who has scrutinized the manuscripts to be certain that I was saying what I wanted to say as well as she knew I could. And then, she has taken words on manuscript pages and transformed them into books that are inviting to read and beautiful to behold. It is she who, in collaboration with Atha Tehon, the art director, and Jane Byers Bierhorst, the designer, decides on typeface, page size, design, layout, kind of paper, and more details than I know. Phyllis and Atha have repeatedly said that the Uncle Remus books have been the most difficult to produce. Whatever the difficulties, Phyllis never sought the easy solution, or even the least expensive. She wanted and obtained only the best solution. Her creative diligence has been indispensable in bringing these tales to a new generation.

Julius Lester
February 25, 1993

Contents

The Last Tales of Uncle Remus

Why the Cricket Has Elbows on His Legs

The first thing you have to understand is that the world today is different than it was back when these stories took place. For one thing, folks were bigger then. My great-grandaddy said his great-grandaddy's great-grandaddy's great-grandaddy was so big that it took three of him to make one of him, if you understand what I'm saying and didn't get lost among the hims. People have swunk up since them days. My great-grandaddy's great-great-grandaddy said it's because folks have stopped eating raw meat and gone to messing with tofu and bean sprouts. That will certainly swunk you up.

In any event, it stands to reason that if the people were bigger, the creatures and the creeping and crawling things were also bigger. And they were! They had bigger houses and if they had bigger houses, then, they had bigger chimneys on the houses. And since that's so, we can proceed to learn about Grandaddy Cricket who, back in the old times, was about goat-size.

During the summer Grandaddy Cricket lived in the woods. He had his fife and his fiddle and he didn't need anything else. One day he would fiddle for the fish to dance. The next he would take out his fife and teach the birds some new tunes.

Over in the autumn, however, when the weather started to get cool, Grandaddy Cricket had to keep his hands in his pockets from early in the morning until close to noontime. By the time he got them warmed up and had played a tune, the sun started going down, on account of the days being shorter. His hands would start getting cold, and he would have to put them back in his pockets before he had finished two tunes.

Well, one year autumn turned to winter and it was the coldest winter there'd ever been in them parts. It was too cold for Grandaddy Cricket to play the fiddle and fife, the dozens, the lottery, or solitaire. He was so cold and hungry all he could do was creep along and try to keep on the sunny side of the world.

That's what he was doing one day when he saw smoke curling into the air. Grandaddy Cricket knew that where there's smoke there is fire. He crept a little faster, and after a while he saw that the smoke was coming from a chimney built at one end of a house.

This house wasn't like the houses you see today. This was an old-timey house. It sat on blocks, which raised it up off the ground, and was made out of logs. The spaces between the logs were stopped up with clay. The chimney, however, was made out of sticks and stones and mud.

Grandaddy Cricket crawled underneath the house, thinking it would be warm there. Not only wasn't it warm, but that was where the wind came to rest when it was out of breath. Ain't nothing colder than the wind setting around huffing and puffing, trying to catch its breath.

Grandaddy Cricket made his way over to the chimney to get some of its warmth. But it was built tight and all the warmth was inside where it was supposed to be.

It didn't take Grandaddy Cricket long to figure out that

if the warmth was inside the chimney, that was where he needed to be too. He gnawed and he sawed, he scratched and he clawed, he pushed and he gouged, he shoved and he scrouged, and after a while he made a hole through the mud-and-rock chimney. Before long Grandaddy Cricket was warm. When Grandaddy Cricket is feeling warm and cozy, he's happy, and when he's happy guess what he has to do?

That's right! Make music!

There wasn't enough room in the crack to play the fiddle, but there was plenty for fife playing, which is what he proceeded to do.

During the day he stopped playing whenever he heard a noise from inside the house. At night, however, when it was dark and the house was quiet, he would play up a storm. The children what lived in the house would lie in their beds and listen and laugh at the happy music. Their father didn't see nothing to be happy about. How could he sleep with all that racket?

Grandaddy Cricket played like he was getting paid for it. Pretty soon he was playing day and night. He played the children off to school in the morning. He played them home at lunchtime. He played to their momma while she baked bread and made soups that didn't have no tofu in them. He played to her when she sat in her rocking chair by the fire and dozed off, dreaming about the times when she was a little girl—the olden times that would make her grandchildren feel funny when they would hear about them.

After a while, the father got tired of all the fifing.

"I'm going to get that cricket out of there."

"You leave that cricket alone," his wife told him. "Crickets are good luck."

"Well, I'd rather have less luck and less fifing," the man yelled into the chimney. "Hush up all that racket!"

Grandaddy Cricket was doing his thing and didn't pay the man no never mind.

"If you don't stop that fifing, I'm going to pour boiling water on you."

Grandaddy Cricket heard *that*. He stopped fifing long enough to sing back:

Hot water will turn me brown,
And then I'll kick your chimney down.

The man said, "We'll see about that."

He put a kettle of water on the fire. When the water was boiling, he took the kettle and poured the scalding water through the cracks in the chimney.

Well, you don't have to be a genius to figure out what happens when you pour water on hard mud. Water plus hard mud will get you soft mud every time. Before the man knew it, the chimney started to sag. As it did, Grandaddy Cricket put his fife in his pocket and started kicking. He kicked and he kicked and the chimney fell down and buried the man.

When the man's wife and children finally dug him out, he was one eyed and splayfooted. His nose was where his ear used to be 'cause his ear was on his lip. His wife and children didn't know him. They had to ask him his name and where he came from and how old he was. After he satisfactorily answered all the questions, the woman said to him, "Didn't I tell you that crickets were good luck?"

"You call this good luck?" the man answered.

Grandaddy Cricket wasn't the same either. He had kicked so hard and kicked so high that he unjointed both of his legs. When he crawled out of the chimney, his elbows were down around his knees, which is where they have stayed.

Grandaddy Cricket didn't mind. He had found himself a home that was cool in the summer and warm in the winter. That's why to this day, crickets live in chimneys.

Why the Earth Is Mostly Water

If you look at a map of the world, you'll see something peculiar. We are surrounded by water and outnumbered by fish!

What kind of sense does that make? If it had been me what made the world, I would've turned the thing around and made more dry than wet. I'm not friendly with water, though I will speak to that in my bathtub every now and then.

Being outnumbered by fish and surrounded by water has always made me nervous, so I did some investigating. I learned that this is not how the Lord first made the world. I always knew the Lord had as much sense as me. He made the world the way I would have—a lot of dry and a little wet. But that's not how things are today.

So what happened? The first thing that happened is that folks got their stories confused. Everybody knows about Noah and the ark and the time it rained forty days and forty nights and the whole world was covered with water. What folks don't know is that that flood was the *second* flood. That's right! There was another flood that happened a long time before Noah was born. Now that I think about it, the flood I'm going to tell you about happened before "Once upon a time." And stories that happened that long ago happened when the animals ruled the world, topside and bottom too.

Back in those days animals had as much sense as people. Maybe more, 'cause people don't have as much sense as they think they do. But back before "Once upon a time," the animals could read and write and do arithmetic, slam dunk a basketball and anything else you can think of.

Once a year the animals had a big convention where they would talk over any problems or grievances they might have with one another. One year the big point of dispute was between the fish and the alligators. Fish said the alligators was moving into the neighborhood and sending it to ruination. Seems like the alligators would sit out on their lawns at night and grunt. Another year the big complaint was about the coyotes and dogs howling at the moon all night and keeping everybody awake.

Well, this particular year the time was at hand for the convention, and the animals come from near and far. The Lion was there, because he was the king. Couldn't be no meeting without him. The Hippopotamus was there, of course. The Elephant came, as did the Giraffe, Griffin, and Pterodactyl. All the animals were there, from the biggest all the way down to the Crawfish.

When everybody was assembled, the Lion shook his mane and roared loud enough to make Jell-O shake. That was the sign for the convention to begin.

The animals started making speeches and screaming and yelling and hollering and cussing and flinging language around like a big wind tossing trees in a storm. Didn't nobody take it too seriously. Animals liked to hear themselves talk same as people.

While all the speech-making was going on, the Elephant

accidently stepped on one of the Crawfish. I don't have to tell you that when an Elephant steps on you, you have been stepped on. When the Elephant lifted up his foot, there was not even a memory of that Crawfish left. To make matters worse, the Elephant didn't even know he had done it.

All the other Crawfish got mad. They had a caucus, which is a little meeting which nobody could come to except Crawfish. They drew up a resolution to protest what the Elephant had done. It was a good resolution too, filled with wherefores and therefores and whereats and be-it-resolveds, and all the other kind of things that make a resolution a resolution and not just a bunch of running off at the mouth.

They got up to read their resolution to the convention, but the Leopards were reading one to the Tigers about the superiority of spots over stripes, and the Hyenas were laughing, and the Beavers were eating all the chairs, and the Snakes were crying because they wanted to hug folks and nobody wanted a hug from them. The Crawfish kept on reading while the Unicorn and the Bull compared horns, and the Cat walked around looking at everybody like they was crazy, and you know what happened? The Elephant squished another Crawfish!

The Crawfish were sho' 'nuf hot now, the few that were left. They drew up another resolution filled with wherefores and therefores and whereats and be-it-resolveds, and tried to read it out to the convention. But that was just the time Brer Rabbit come by selling the latest issue of *Animal* magazine. I don't remember who was on the cover. It could've been Jackie Opossum. Naw, I believe it was Michael Jackass. Then again it could've been Madonna

Llama. Well, whoever it was, everybody got so excited that it busted up the convention for that day.

The Crawfish were seriously upset now! You can do a lot of things wrong in this life, but don't ever cross swords with a mad crawfish. It might be one of the littlest things in the world, but 'cause something is little don't mean it ain't powerful. That's what the animals were about to find out.

The Crawfish nodded to their cousins, the Mud Turtles. The Mud Turtles nodded to their cousins, the Spring Lizards. All of them together started boring holes in the earth. Down and down and down into the earth they went, all the way to the center.

Back in that time that's where the water was. But after the Crawfish and the Mud Turtles and the Spring Lizards got through boring all them holes, that is not where the water stayed. No, indeed! Them little creatures unloosed all the fountains in the earth!

The water started spouting up out of the earth, and it spewed and it spewed and it spewed. Noah thought he saw something when it rained forty days and forty nights. Shucks, Noah didn't know what water was. The water he saw was coming from on high. The water the Crawfish, Mud Turtles, and Spring Lizards let loose was from within, and it spouted out of the center of the world for three months, seventeen days, and forty-'leven minutes.

Finally the rain stopped, and as far as the eye could see, water covered everything. It covered the tallest trees; it covered the tallest trees on the tallest mountains, and even some low-flying clouds. For a few days, the Almighty thought He might have to raise heaven's skirts up.

Well, quite naturally, all the animals drowned, all of them, that is except the Mud Turtles, Spring Lizards, Crawfish, and all the other kinds of fish. The Earth animals died because they thought they was too big to listen to something as little as the Crawfish.

So, the Lord had to make the world all over again. This time He decided to put most of the water on *top* of the earth instead of inside.

Which is why most of the world is water today. If the Crawfish ever get mad again and bore down to the center of the world, they are going to be in for a surprise. Nothing down there now but fire.

The Origin of the Ocean

Some folks say the story I just told you is not the real one of why the world is mostly water. There's another story that also explains the matter. Sometimes things are so perplexing that one story don't satisfy everybody. That's fine with me, 'cause it means another story.

It used to be that all the animals lived on the same side of the world. That's because the world only had one side, and that was all over. Wasn't no oceans separating folks. Back in those times you would've found tigers in Toledo, lions in Louisville, apes in Arkadelphia, and baboons in Boston. It probably would've stayed that way too if Brer Lion hadn't messed with Brer Rabbit.

One day Brer Lion decided to go hunting and he asked Brer Rabbit to go with him. Brer Rabbit was ready for every kind of fun on the topside of the ground.

Off they went. Whenever they found some game, Brer Lion would leap at it but would miss. Brer Rabbit would chase it down and catch it. The instant he did Brer Lion roared, "It's mine! It's mine! I killed it!"

Brer Lion was so big that Brer Rabbit wasn't about to dispute him. But Brer Rabbit didn't forget. All that day Brer Lion would leap at the game and miss. Brer Rabbit would catch it and Brer Lion would roar, "It's mine! It's mine! I killed it!"

That evening they were so far from home they had to camp out next to a creek. They built a fire, cooked their supper, and afterward sat around the fire. Brer Rabbit started bragging long and loud about what a great hunter Brer Lion was. Brer Lion leaned back on his elbows and swelled up with pride.

Brer Rabbit bragged so hard, he soon wore himself out. He yawned. "I believe it's time to get some shut-eye, Brer Lion. You may be a powerful hunter, but when it comes to sleeping, I don't know as there is a creature in creation that can do more serious sleeping than me. So, I'm going to apologize in advance for disturbing your rest."

Brer Lion was insulted. "Don't be too sure, Brer Rabbit. When it comes to sleeping, I ain't no amateur."

Brer Rabbit was doubtful. "What do you sound like just as you're falling asleep?"

Brer Lion made a sound like a saw sawing trees.

"And what do you sound like after you're sleeping good?"

The noise that came out of Brer Lion sounded like a mountain falling down. Brer Rabbit was amazed. "That's some sho' 'nuf sleeping you be doing, Brer Lion."

"I'm the king, ain't I?"

"That you are. That you are."

Brer Lion smiled, stretched out on his side, and soon he was snoring like he snored when he wasn't too far asleep.

Brer Rabbit listened.

After a while it started to sound like a mountain was falling down. Brer Rabbit knew Brer Lion was sho' 'nuf asleep.

Brer Rabbit went to the fire. He took cold ashes and sprinkled them on himself. Then he took some hot coals out of the fire and threw them on Brer Lion.

Brer Lion jumped up. "Who did that? Who did that?"

Brer Rabbit was lying on the ground, kicking and screaming and yelling, "Ow! Ow! OW!"

Brer Lion saw Brer Rabbit covered with ashes and kicking and squalling like he was burning alive. It was obvious somebody had tried to set both of them on fire. Brer Lion peered into the darkness but didn't see anybody.

He lay down and was soon asleep, mountain after mountain crumbling.

Brer Rabbit went to the fire. He sprinkled cold ashes on himself, then threw hot coals on Brer Lion again.

Brer Lion jumped up, screaming. Brer Rabbit lay on the ground, kicking and squawking, "Ow! Ow! OW!"

When Brer Rabbit caught his breath, he got up and looked at Brer Lion. "You ought to be ashamed, trying to burn me up like that."

Brer Lion held up his hands. "Wasn't me, Brer Rabbit. I swear it wasn't."

Brer Rabbit looked like he didn't believe him. Then, he sniffed the air. "I smell rags burning."

Brer Lion sniffed. "Me too." He smelled some more. The more he smelled, the closer the odor. The more he smelled, the warmer he got. "That ain't rags. That's my hair!" He rolled on the ground and put the fire out and fell back to sleep. Soon, the mountains started falling again.

Brer Rabbit got up and sprinkled himself with cold ashes and threw hot coals on Brer Lion.

As Brer Lion jumped up, Brer Rabbit was hollering, "I saw him, Brer Lion. I saw him. He came from across the creek. He sho' did!"

Brer Lion roared a roaracious roar and jumped across the creek. As soon as he did, Brer Rabbit cut the string that held the two banks of the creek together.

When he cut the string, the banks of the creek began to fall away from each other. They got farther and farther and farther away, and the creek got wider and wider and wider. After a while it was so wide that Brer Rabbit couldn't see Brer Lion and Brer Lion couldn't see Brer Rabbit. It got so wide that Brer Rabbit couldn't even see land. And neither could Brer Lion. All the animals that was on one side with Brer Lion had to stay there, and all them what was on the same side as Brer Rabbit had to stay there. And that's where they been from that day to this, with the big water rolling between.

Now, I know what you're thinking. How could the banks of the creek be tied together with a string? Well, it's a strange thing about stories. You have to take them as you get them. But I promise you this: The next time the Tale Teller comes through here, I'll ask him. If you aren't too far away, I'll send word for you to come quick and you can hear what the Tale Teller has to say about that. So, don't be getting upset with me 'cause I don't know how the creeks could be tied together with a string. Who put the string there, I don't know about that either. But I do know who cut the string. I sure do!

––––––––––––

Brer Rabbit and Miss Nancy

There have been three periods in the life of the world. There was the time before people. That's when the animals were in charge of everything.

Then there was the time when people and animals lived with each other like there wasn't no difference between them. People could understand animal talk, and the animals could understand people talk, and it was hard to tell who was animal and who was person.

Finally, there's today, when the people are in charge of everything. To my mind the world was a lot better off when the people and the animals lived with each other like everybody was part of the same family.

For instance, back then there were easy times and hard ones just like today. One year the economics turned bad. First there was a recession, and then the recession got depressed and by the time the recession took its depression to a therapist, well, hardly anybody could find a job. Brer Rabbit felt very lucky the day Mr. Man offered him one.

"I can't pay you, but you can eat for free."

"That's payment enough!" Brer Rabbit responded.

Brer Rabbit worked hard, hoeing potatoes, chopping cotton, weeding the vegetables. Mr. Man said that Brer Rabbit was one of the best workers he'd ever had. He told his daughter that if she wanted to marry somebody who wasn't afraid of hard work, Brer Rabbit was the man.

Well, one hot day Brer Rabbit had been working out in the sun for a long time and he was hungry and thirsty.

"It's hot today!"

Mr. Man agreed. "Well, there's the bucket and you know where the creek is. Go get yourself a drink."

Brer Rabbit filled the bucket and drank it empty. However, all that water and no food made his stomach mad. It started growling and complaining: "Give me some food! I want some food!"

Brer Rabbit's stomach was growling and fussing so loud that Mr. Man heard it. "Go on up to the house and tell my daughter to give you some bread."

Brer Rabbit went up to the house and knocked on the door. When Mr. Man's daughter saw who it was, she said, "Why, Brer Rabbit! What're you doing here? My daddy said that you are the best worker he has, but if you call standing out here on the porch working, I think there's something wrong with my daddy's eyesight."

"I'm here, Miss Nancy, because your daddy sent me."

"And why would he send you up here?"

"He sent me to get two dollars and some bread and butter."

Miss Nancy gave Brer Rabbit a suspicious look. "I don't believe you. I'm going to ask Daddy about this."

Before Brer Rabbit could say a word, Miss Nancy was running down the path to the field. "Daddy! Is you say what Brer Rabbit say you say?"

Mr. Man yelled back, "That's what I said!"

Miss Nancy went back to the house and gave Brer Rabbit two dollars and some bread and butter.

A few hours later Brer Rabbit went up to the house and asked Miss Nancy for two more dollars and some bread and butter. She went to the field and asked her daddy, "Is you say what Brer Rabbit say you say?" Her daddy said that he had. She gave Brer Rabbit two more dollars and some bread and butter.

This went on for some days. Mr. Man was almost out of money and didn't know it. However, Brer Rabbit knew that one day soon Mr. Man would look in his money box and see more box than money.

Well, it just so happened that Miss Nancy had a new boyfriend. I don't remember what his name was. Seems I heard my great-granddaddy tell my great-uncle's nephew's cousin's wife that his name was Doofus McGoofus. Whatever his name was, Brer Rabbit didn't like him. And if Brer Rabbit don't like you, you are in trouble. Sometimes you in trouble if he does like you.

One day Mr. Man and Brer Rabbit were working in the field together. Mr. Man heard Brer Rabbit talking under his breath, but he couldn't make out the words.

"Brer Rabbit? What're you talking about?"

"Who? Me?"

"Ain't nobody else here."

Brer Rabbit looked around like he wasn't quite sure. "I was just concentrating on learning a song I heard a blue jay singing this morning." Brer Rabbit went back to hoeing and mumbling.

This didn't satisfy Mr. Man. "What did the blue jay sing?"

Brer Rabbit stopped, scratched his head, and squinted. "I believe it went something like this:

> *The boy kissed the girl and called her honey;*
> *He kissed her again and she gave him all the money.*

"What money?" Mr. Man wanted to know.

"How should I know?" Brer Rabbit answered. "I'm not in the song. Anyway, it's just a song."

But Mr. Man couldn't get the song out of his mind:

> *The boy kissed the girl and called her honey;*
> *He kissed her again and she gave him all the money.*

The song went round and round in Mr. Man's head. The more times it went round, the more worried he got.

That evening when he went home, Doofus McGoofus was sitting on the porch with Miss Nancy. Mr. Man said a polite "Howdy do" and went in the house. He didn't go to the kitchen to wash his hands like he usually did. He went straight to his office, opened the cabinet, and took out his money box. He looked inside and it was almost empty!

"Where's my money?" he yelled, running onto the porch.

Miss Nancy said she didn't know.

"Yes you do!" Mr. Man declared. "You gave almost all

my money to Doofus. Pack your things and you and Doofus get out of here right now!"

Miss Nancy pleaded and cried. Mr. Man would not change his mind. So Miss Nancy packed up her things and went on off with Doofus.

As for Brer Rabbit and Mr. Man—well, Brer Rabbit was just being Brer Rabbit. Faulting him for that would be like faulting winter for being cold. Can't say as much for Mr. Man, though. But, that's how men can be—adding two and two and coming up with seventy-seven.

The Old King and the New King

Nothing in this world will get you in trouble quicker than your mouth. A lot of times your mouth goes in motion while your brain is still asleep. Other times your brain is telling you to say, "No," and your mouth says, "Yes." But even if your mouth and brain are good friends, don't go to thinking that you're as smart as God. There's always somebody else whose mouth and brains are like twins.

That's what happened, this king learned.

I don't know whether the king had a name. He probably did when he was a baby, but once he became king, well, that's what everybody called him. After a while even he forgot his name. So, if *he* thought his name was king, we don't have any reason to think it was Junebug Jabbo Jones.

The other thing that's not in the story is where he did his kinging. It could've been in Zimbabwe, Zanzibar, or Zululand. Then again, he might have been king in Cambodia, Canada, or Cameroon. But who knows? He also could've been king in Des Moines, Dubuque, or Dallas. But the story don't say where he was king at, so anyplace you put him is all right with me and him.

The king had been kinging for a long time. Seemed like he started kinging before water was wet. He had been kinging so long that his hair had fallen out, all his teeth were loose, and his toenails had whiskers. Worst of all, his brain and his mouth had not spoken to one another in many years.

It was time for a new king. There were things that needed deciding, such as whether the grass in the kingdom should be painted yellow and orange like some folks wanted. Another decision to be made was whether folks should breathe through both nostrils at the same time or breathe through the right one on Monday, Wednesday, and Friday, the left one on Tuesday, Thursday, and Saturday, and breathe how they wanted on Sunday.

A delegation went to the king.

"King? We don't want to hurt your feelings, but it is time for somebody else to do the kinging."

The king listened. The more he listened, the tighter he sat in his chair. That night, the king didn't go to bed, but slept in his throne chair. The next day he ate all his meals in his throne chair. It was obvious he was not going to get off the throne until he died.

The people decided they couldn't wait for that. They had a large meeting, and everybody agreed on who would make the best king. They went to the person and asked him to be the new king. He said he would.

The delegation went to the palace and told the old king that he had to make room for the new king.

"Who is he?" the old king wanted to know.

Nobody said anything. The old king might kill him if he knew.

"Is he an old man?" the king wanted to know.

If the king thought the new king was old, he would have all the old people killed. If he thought the new king was young, he would have all the young people killed.

"Older than some and younger than others," somebody responded.

The king got angry. He roared and he yelled and he screamed and he threatened. But no one would tell him who the new king was going to be.

The king got very quiet. Finally, he said, "You think I don't have any sense. Well, tell this new king that before he can be king he has to send me a beef. But it can't be a bull and it can't be a cow. When he can do that, then I'll know he has sense enough to be king."

How could there be meat that was not from a bull or a cow? The man chosen to be king was a young man. Maybe he didn't have enough sense to be king if answering questions like this was what kinging was about.

The delegation went to see the young man they wanted to be king.

"The old king said you can be king if you send him some beef that is not from a bull or a cow."

The young man smiled and winked one eye. "Tell the old king that I've got a steer in my pen, but he has to come and get it. And he can't come in the day and he can't come at night."

They ran back to the palace and told the old king what the young man had said.

The king scratched his head. He scratched his stomach. He scratched in his armpits. But wherever he scratched, he couldn't come up with an answer. So, he took off his crown and his robe and walked out the door and down the road.

It just goes to show that your mouth and your brain might make folks believe water is running backward. But there's always somebody who can make 'em believe water can dance.

And don't *ever* forget: There is always somebody younger right outside the door.

Brer Bear Comes to the Community

Brer Bear didn't always live with the other animals. He was born and raised way off in the woods with his family. His daddy taught him all he needed to know—how to rob a bee tree and dig for sweet potatoes, get roasting ears off a cornstalk, and whatever else he needed to know.

Brer Bear decided he wanted to see what was on the other side of the woods. When the day came for him to go, his father gave him seven pieces of honey in the comb. "I don't have much to give you, but this will be more than enough. Whoever eats a piece of that honey will have to wrestle you every morning for seven years and give you everything he has."

Brer Bear put the seven pieces of honeycomb in his bag, slung the bag on his back, and went his way. He walked all that day. When night came, he made camp and went to sleep.

The next morning he had scarcely gotten his eyes open

when he heard a rustling in the bushes. It was Brer Tiger looking for his breakfast.

Brer Bear howdied Brer Tiger. Brer Tiger howdied back.

Brer Bear opened his bag, took out a piece of the honeycomb, and started eating.

Brer Tiger watched. Brer Bear knew Brer Tiger was hungry. "I would invite you to join me in eating some of this honeycomb, but whoever eats it will have to wrestle me every morning for seven years and give me all their possessions."

"I'm a very good wrestler," Brer Tiger responded. "And I'm also very hungry."

Brer Bear shrugged. "Don't say I didn't warn you."

Brer Tiger grinned and proceeded to eat his fill of honey. "This honey is so good I'll wrestle you eleven years."

After a while Brer Tiger had his fill of honey. He thanked Brer Bear and headed for home. He didn't get very far, though, before he felt a zooming in his head and a crawling on his hide. It got so bad that all he wanted to do was to go back to Brer Bear.

When he got there Brer Bear was curled up taking a nap.

"Wake up!" Brer Tiger shouted. "I feel like wrestling!"

Brer Bear put his grin on and it looked like it fit him. "You can have all the underholds, Brer Tiger, and you got to promise not to use the inturn, the hamtwist, and the kneelock."

Brer Tiger didn't know what Brer Bear was talking about. But he found out when Brer Bear grabbed him, swung him around and around, snorted in his face, squeezed him tight, hit him in the head, and then lay on top of him.

Brer Tiger's pants were split, and his head felt as big as the moon. He limped home and went to bed.

Early the next morning Brer Tiger heard a knock at his door. He looked out, and there was Brer Bear standing on the doorstep. "I come to wrestle you. We got six years and three hundred and sixty-four days to go."

Brer Tiger went outside, and Brer Bear twirled him around in the air, slammed him down on his back, jumped on his midsection a time or two, twisted his legs around, bit his ear, and fell on top of him.

When Brer Tiger got up, didn't a soul recognize him except his wife and Brer Rabbit.

Brer Rabbit shook his head and said, "Brer Tiger, what you need is a change of scenery."

Brer Tiger agreed that was so. He moved out of his house and didn't take a thing with him. Brer Bear moved in, took over all Brer Tiger's possessions and has been living with the animals ever since.

The Snake

Once there was a woman by the name of Coomba. Some say she was from Africa.

One day she went for a walk through the woods. She happened on a Snake nest with an egg in it. A very big Snake sat atop the egg, and it was a very big egg.

Coomba thought about the omelet she could make from an egg that size. But the Snake was looking at her like it knew what she was thinking and that her thinking included the green peppers, onions, and cheese she would put in the omelet.

Coomba looked at the Snake.

Snake looked at Coomba.

Coomba decided to let the egg stay where it was.

But it's a strange thing when something gets in your mind. You can't forget it, no matter how hard you try. Whatever Coomba did, the thought of that egg followed her like it was her shadow. Wherever she went, the egg was there too, beckoning, beckoning.

The next morning Coomba hurried through the woods and across the field and hid behind a tree until she saw the Snake slide away to go hunt its breakfast.

Coomba grabbed the egg and hurried home. Before King

Sun had finished gathering the dew to make his morning coffee, Coomba had cooked the egg and eaten it.

When the Snake came back to its nest and saw that the egg was gone, it put its nose on the ground and followed the scent to Coomba's house.

"Where's my egg?" the Snake asked plaintively.

"I haven't seen your egg," Coomba responded.

Snake saw the snakeskin which had been over the egg hanging from a nail on the wall. "What is that?"

Coomba didn't say anything.

"Why did you take my egg?"

Coomba pretended like she hadn't heard the Snake.

"You hear my voice crying out," the Snake said. "You took my egg. You destroyed my children. Take care of your own, woman. Take care of your own."

Snake left.

Time passed. Coomba gave birth to a little girl whom she called Noncy. Coomba didn't know she could love anything as much as she loved that little girl. Coomba loved her hard and everywhere Coomba went, she carried Noncy next to her.

As soon as Noncy was born, however, Snake hid itself in the grass outside Coomba's house. Snake watched all day. Snake watched all night, its tongue flickering in and out, in and out.

Snake waited.

Noncy grew. Noncy grew until she was too big to carry. "I can't carry you with me anymore when I go out to work in the fields. And you are too young to come and not get in the way. I must leave you at home."

Coomba showed Noncy how to lock the door. "When I come home, I will sing this song:

Walla walla witto, me Noncy,
Walla walla witto, me Noncy,
Walla walla witto, me Noncy!

When I do, you sing:

Andolee! Andoli! Andolo!

And then you open the door."

Snake lay in the grass, listening.

Throughout the day, every day, Coomba came home from the field to be sure Noncy was all right. Each time she sang:

Walla walla witto, me Noncy,
Walla walla witto, me Noncy,
Walla walla witto, me Noncy!

And from inside came:

Andolee! Andoli! Andolo!

The door would open and Coomba would go inside.

After listening for several days, Snake slid up to Coomba's door one morning after she left.

Wullo wullo widdo, me Noncy,
Wullo wullo widdo, me Noncy,
Wullo wullo widdo, me Noncy!

Snake tried to make its voice like Coomba's, but Snake's voice sounded like graveyard dirt rattling in a tin can. Noncy didn't say a word.

"Open the door," Snake yelled.

"My momma don't holler like that," Noncy replied.

Snake tried to sing the song again, but Noncy was quiet. Snake tried and tried. No luck. Finally, Snake flickered its tongue and slid away.

Soon, Coomba came.

> *Walla walla witto, me Noncy,*
> *Walla walla witto, me Noncy,*
> *Walla walla witto, me Noncy!*

Noncy said, "That's my momma." And she sang:

> *Andolee! Andoli! Andolo!*

Snake listened closely and practiced hard.

The next morning when Coomba went to the fields, Snake slid up to the door and sang:

> *Walla walla witto, me Noncy,*
> *Walla walla witto, me Noncy,*
> *Walla walla witto, me Noncy!*

Noncy thought it was her mother and she sang:

> *Andolee! Andoli! Andolo!*

She opened the door and Snake swished inside like a cold wind. Snake hugged the little girl and twisted its tail around her, twisted and twisted until Snake was coiled around Noncy from toe to head.

Noncy hollered and screamed and squalled.

Snake squeezed and squeezed until Noncy was as thin as a tear. Then, it swallowed her whole.

When Coomba came home, she sang out. No song came back. She sang louder. The silence came back louder.

Coomba touched the door. It opened when it should have been locked. She looked inside. The house was empty. Coomba stood in the doorway, wondering where her daughter could be.

Then she looked down. There, in the dust, were the swirling grooves left by Snake.

"Oh, no!"

Coomba went to the swamp and cut a piece of cane. Then, she followed the snake track.

Snake was so full carrying Noncy inside that it could not go fast. Snake was so full carrying Noncy inside that it became sleepy. Soon it was not moving at all.

When Coomba caught up to Snake, it was lying in the path, asleep. Coomba hit Snake over the head with the piece of cane until its head was as flat as a broken promise.

Then she cut Snake open. There, inside, was Noncy, sound asleep.

Coomba took her home and washed her clean. Noncy opened her eyes, saw her mother, and sang:

Andolee! Andoli! Andolo!

And Coomba and Noncy lived happily for many, many years.

A Ghost Story

Some folks don't believe in ghosts, which is fine with me. You believe what you believe.

However, if you had seen all that I have seen since I peeped out of the womb, you would be as nice to the dead as you are to the living. Maybe nicer.

Once there was a man and a woman. If they had names, I don't recollect what they were. Could've been Rick and Ilse, or Rock and Doris, Fred and Wilma, or Homer and Marge. Names didn't count for as much back in them times, so it don't make no never mind. If you need them to have names, you stick them on. I don't, so I'll just call 'em a man and a woman.

They grew up together in the same community and liked one another since they were little things. Everybody knew that when they got grown, they would marry one another. Strange thing was that they didn't.

I don't know why. They probably didn't either. Maybe he never asked her. Maybe there wasn't a reason. There ain't a reason for everything, you know. Some things are because they are and other things ain't because they ain't.

Just as no one knows how come the two of them didn't get married, nobody knows how come the woman's health began to fail. One day she took to her sickbed. Wasn't long before her sickbed became her deathbed.

In a community as small as that one, there wasn't no undertaker to do things for folks. Folks did everything for themselves.

When the woman breathed her last breath, folks laid her out real pretty and lighted some candles and put them at her head. They put two big round silver dollars on her eyes to keep them shut. Don't nothing mess with your appetite like having a dead person staring at you.

Folks told the man that since he knew the woman better than anyone, he should go dig her grave and bury her.

The man took the body out to the cemetery and dug her grave. Just as he was about to put her in the ground he saw those silver dollars on her eyelids, shining like hope.

He picked one up. It felt good in his fingers. He picked up the other one. It felt good too.

The woman's eyes opened. She was staring at him. Quickly, he threw her body in the grave and covered it with dirt. The two silver dollars were jingling and jangling in his pocket.

He hurried home and put the two coins in a tin box. He shook the box. The money jingled like it was music. But the man didn't feel so good. Regardless of where he looked, regardless of whether his eyes were open or closed, the woman seemed to be staring at him. The man decided to go to bed early.

He hadn't been asleep long, before the wind began to

rise. At first it was a small wind and made a small sound—
Woooooo—as if it were just being born.

But the wind got stronger and stronger and louder and
louder.

WOOOOO! It blew on top of the house.

WOOOOOO! It blew under the house.

WOOOOOO! WOOOOO! It blew on all four sides of
the house.

WOOOOOOOOOOOOOOOOOOOOOOOOOOOO-
OOOOOOOOOOOOOOOO!

"Ain't nothing but the wind," he told himself, and tried
to go back to sleep.

The wind hollered and cried. It blew on top of the house.
It blew under the house. It blew on all four sides of the
house. And it found the cracks in the walls and whistled,
EEEEEEEEEEEEEEEEEEEEEEEEEEEEEEEEEEEE-
EEEEE!

The man started trembling and shaking. Then, he heard
something at his money box.

Clinkity, clinkalinkle!

"Hey! Who's stealing my money?"

OOOOOOOOOOO! EEEEEEEEEEEE!

Clinkity, clinkalinkle!

The man got out of bed and looked around. He didn't
see anything. He double-locked the door and went back
to bed.

His head had just touched the pillow when—*Clinkity,
clinkalinkle!*

"Must be a rat in my money box," the man said.

He got out of bed again and looked at his money box
on the mantelpiece. It was closed tightly.

He opened it. The two silver dollars shone like dreams.

He closed the box, and as he put it down there came a voice:

"Where's my money?"

Clinkity, clinkalinkle, clink!

"Where's my money?"

The man put a chair against the front door. Then he jumped in bed and pulled the covers over his head.

Clinkity, clinkalinkle, clink!

"Where's my money?"

The man shook and the man shivered; the money clinked and clanked; the voice came nearer and nearer.

"Where's my money?"

"WHERE'S MY MONEY?"

"WHERE'S MY MONEY?"

The front door flew open. The chair the man had stacked against it went tumbling across the floor.

The man peeped over the covers. It was the woman!

Clinkity, clinkalinkle, clink!

"Where's my money?"

"Oh Lordy, Lordy, Lord," said the man.

The woman groped through the room touching the table and the chairs and the wall. She got close to the bed and felt the mattress. Then she jumped on the man and hollered, "YOU HAVE MY MONEY!"

The next morning folks found the man just as dead as dead can get. They laid him out like they had the woman and thought it would be nice to put him in the same grave with her. Now they could be together as folks had thought they should've been.

The man didn't have to give up the silver dollars, though. Except this time, they were on *his* eyes.

Brer Bear Exposes Brer Rabbit

One Saturday when all the creatures had finished their work for the week, they were sitting around talking politics. When they had solved all the problems in the world, which is easy to do when you ain't got none of the responsibility, they got to talking about which one of them could eat the most.

Brag breeds brag. Brer Wolf said, "I don't know how much I can eat because there has never been a day when I've been able to eat as much as I wanted to."

Brer Bear said, "I could eat a horse if I had enough salt."

Brer Fox said, "I'll match any man here, chew for chew and swallow for swallow."

Brer Rabbit was laying back with his eyes closed. They heard him chuckle. "If you will buy the food, I guarantee you that I'll eat more than all of you put together. If I don't, I'll give you my hat."

I don't know what was so special about Brer Rabbit's hat that anybody else would want it, but the animals agreed to the deal.

The next Saturday they got together for a big barbecue. They had hogs and they had sheep and they had cows and they barbecued all the meat and were ready for the eating contest to begin. They looked around for Brer Rabbit and didn't see him.

"Where's Brer Rabbit?" they wondered.

Just about then they saw Brer Rabbit coming across the hill. He had on a long cloak and was walking with a cane, walking slow like he had gotten old between moondown and sunrise.

"I'm sick. Mighty sick. If I was a little more sick, I would not have gotten this far in the world."

"What's the matter, Brer Rabbit?"

"I got a headache. I got a backache. I went down in the swamp after some calamus root and got my feet wet. That gave me a bad cold and the cold flew to my head, spread to my back, dropped down in my legs, and I almost died."

By the time Brer Rabbit finished telling everybody how his coporosity come to be segashuating that way, the creatures were very suspicious. And why wouldn't they be? He had tricked each of them and more than once.

"If you're so sick, how can you beat us eating?" they wanted to know.

Brer Rabbit sighed. "It's a fact that I'm feeling bad and my pulse is slow and I ain't got no appetite and I can hardly stand up on three legs, but I didn't want nobody to think I was trying to get out of nothing and that's why I came. If I can't beat you eating, that's how it is. But if I can, then I will."

The creatures were satisfied.

They took all the meat and piled it on a long table, making the biggest pile in front of Brer Rabbit. Brer Rabbit bent over backward to see the top, and it was in the clouds.

"Don't forget," Brer Rabbit said, "you got to eat the meat and the bones."

The creatures looked at one another. "The bones?"

"Bones!" Brer Rabbit repeated.

They started into eating. Brer Rabbit was going at it so fast that he made a blur. Before anybody had had a good belch, Brer Rabbit was done and talking about how hungry he was. They gave him more meat and he started in on that.

Brer Bear was sitting off to the side. He had one eye on Brer Rabbit and saw him drop meat in his cloak. Brer Bear didn't say a word. He waited.

After a while, all the meat was gone, and the creatures agreed that Brer Rabbit had outeaten everybody. Brer Bear walked over to Brer Rabbit like he was going to shake his hand. Instead he reached out and grabbed Brer Rabbit's cloak and pulled it off. Hidden inside the cloak was a great big bag. In the bag was all the meat Brer Rabbit was supposed to have eaten.

Brer Rabbit didn't wait around. He dropped his cane and dashed into the bushes.

The creatures might could outeat Brer Rabbit, but there was no way they were going to outrun him.

Brer Rabbit Teaches Brer Bear to Comb His Hair

Brer Bear shouldn't have done what he did. Brer Rabbit was just having fun. He wasn't going to hurt nobody by playing that trick. But when Brer Bear exposed him like that, Brer Rabbit decided to teach Brer Bear a lesson.

Brer Rabbit took to primping himself every day. He put grease in his hair and slicked it down real slick. He put on cologne. He was gleaming like sunlight on dew and smelling like honeysuckle in May, and every morning he went and promenaded past Brer Bear's house.

Miz Bear would be outdoors hanging up clothes on the

line or working in her garden. When she saw Brer Rabbit, he would tip his hat and bow, as polite as he could be.

Miz Bear saw how nice Brer Rabbit looked and she started taking closer looks at Brer Bear. His hair was matted and tangled, and he smelled like a, well, like a *bear*!

"How come you don't look nice like Brer Rabbit?" she asked.

"I don't want to look like that scoundrel."

"Scoundrel or not, ain't nothing wrong with having your hair combed. You look like a rat's bed."

Brer Bear's feelings were hurt. He didn't want his wife thinking Brer Rabbit was more handsome than he was. One day he saw Brer Rabbit going along the road and asked him, "How do you keep your hair so slick?"

Brer Rabbit said, "I don't comb my hair, Brer Bear."

"You don't? Then, how do you do it?"

"My wife does it for me. She combs my head every morning."

"She does? How does she get it to lay down and gleam like that?"

"She takes the axe and chops the hair off. That's so she can get at it good and have it separate out. Then she puts it back on and there it is, all combed."

Brer Bear thought that over for a minute. "Don't it hurt?"

"Hurt? I ain't no coward!"

Bear Bear thought some more. "Don't it make your head bleed?"

"What's a little blood if it means keeping up appearances?"

Brer Bear nodded.

He went home and told Miz Bear how Brer Rabbit combed his hair. Miz Bear got the axe. Brer Bear put his head down on a log. Miz Bear raised the axe up high. Brer Bear closed his eyes and hollered, "Cut if off easy!"

WHOP!

And that took care of Brer Bear. If it had been me, I would let Brer Rabbit have that meat. I sho' would have.

Why Brer Possum Has No Hair on His Tail

There aren't too many tales about Brer Possum. That's because he never did that much. Why would he? Brer Possum is one of the laziest animals in creation. One time, though, his laziness got him in trouble.

On this particular day Brer Possum woke up hungry. If you and I wake up hungry, we go to the refrigerator, get a slice of cold pizza, and tell our stomachs that it is time to go to work. Brer Possum woke up hungry and did not know what to do. He hung there in the tree, upside down, his tail curled around a limb, listening to his stomach. His stomach was saying, "Fool! Go find some cold pizza!"

Brer Possum was too lazy to go anywhere. He thought if he hung there long enough, food would come to him. He changed his mind, however, when he overheard his stomach tell Ol' Man Death, "Come get this fool!" Brer Possum decided it was time to do something.

He dropped out of the tree at the very minute Brer Rabbit was walking by, and almost landed on him.

"You trying to hit me?" Brer Rabbit hollered angrily.

"No, no, Brer Rabbit. Why would I do that? You and me always been the best of friends."

"That's true," Brer Rabbit agreed. "So tell me. How you be?"

"I'm hungry," said Brer Possum.

"A body has to be smart to keep a full stomach these days," Brer Rabbit agreed. "But I believe I know where you can get as much to eat as you want."

"Where's that?" Brer Possum asked eagerly.

"Brer Bear's apple orchard. Brer Bear don't care nothing about apples. He's a honey man. He watches the bees when they come to the apple blossoms. When the bees leave he follows them to their hive and gets the honey."

Brer Possum lit out for Brer Bear's apple orchard. Sure enough, the trees were full of the reddest, juiciest apples you can imagine. Brer Possum climbed to the top of the biggest tree and proceeded to do away with some apples.

While Brer Possum was getting fat on the apples, what do you think Brer Rabbit was doing? He was banging on Brer Bear's door.

"Brer Bear! Brer Bear! There's somebody in your apple trees."

Brer Bear came barreling out of the house. He couldn't afford to have somebody eating his apples. That's what he filled up on before he went into hibernation every winter. He lit out for the apple orchard.

Brer Possum thought he heard somebody coming. "Just one more apple."

He ate another one. He heard something again, and it was closer this time.

"Just one more."

The noise was closer now. Brer Possum looked out over the landscape and there was Brer Bear running toward the orchard like a runaway horse.

"Just one more," said Brer Possum.

That was one more too many.

Brer Possum was still chewing when Brer Bear started shaking the tree with all his strength, and down came Brer Possum like a leaf in a November wind.

But Brer Possum's feet were moving before he touched the ground, and when he did, those little legs shot him five feet down the road.

Brer Bear took off after him. Brer Bear may be big but he ain't slow. Uh-uh. It wasn't long before Brer Bear caught up to Brer Possum and grabbed him.

That didn't mean a thing to Brer Possum. Caught or not, Brer Possum didn't stop moving his legs. They were churning and turning and kicking up grass so bad that Brer Bear's grip was slipping. He bent over and grabbed Brer Possum's tail in his teeth.

That didn't slow Brer Possum down either. His little legs were still flinging dirt and grass back into Brer Bear's eyes. Brer Possum kicked and scratched and scratched and kicked until you would have thought a little tornado had landed. He kicked and scratched until he kicked and scratched his tail right out of Brer Bear's teeth. And all the hair on his tail came off in Brer Bear's mouth.

Brer Bear started coughing and gagging and he might've strangulated to death if Brer Rabbit hadn't come along and beat him on the back until Brer Possum's hair came out of his throat.

The hair may have come out of Brer Bear's throat, but it didn't go back on Brer Possum's tail. That's why, from that day to this, the Possum has no hair on his tail.

Why Brer Possum Loves Peace

Brer Possum might've had a naked tail, but it didn't seem to embarrass him. Neither did it make much difference to his best friend, Brer Coon.

Brer Possum and Brer Coon were about the best buddies that could be. They got together every day to chat about this, that, and the other, and every evening, just before the stars came out, they took a little stroll through the neighborhood.

One evening they were out strolling when they met Brer Dog, who was out taking *his* stroll. He didn't like them and they didn't like him.

Brer Possum and Brer Coon always gave Brer Dog as

much room as he wanted. This evening, however, they looked this way and that way and there wasn't much room to give Brer Dog.

"What we gon' do if he comes for us?" Brer Coon asked.

Brer Possum laughed. "Nothing to worry about. If he comes, I'll stand by you. What you want to do?"

"Only one thing to do. If he runs up on me, I'll make him wish he'd stayed home and scratched his fleas."

The words had hardly covered the distance from his mouth to Brer Possum's ears before Brer Dog ran straight for them.

Brer Dog swung at Brer Possum's stomach. Brer Possum giggled and fell over like he was dead. Brer Dog then went after Brer Coon. That was where he made his mistake.

Brer Coon grabbed Brer Dog and turned him ever-which-a-way-but-loose. He kung fued his eyeballs; he judoed his tail, jujitsued his ears, sat on his wet nose, and karated his bow-wow. Have mercy! Brer Dog felt worse than he did the time he ate a pepperoni, green pepper, anchovy, onion, and sauerkraut pizza for breakfast. He ran away from there so fast, his shadow had to hitchhike home.

Brer Coon was feeling pretty good until he looked down and saw Brer Possum lying on the ground like he was dead. After a minute or so, Brer Possum raised up, gave a weak grin, and ran off.

A couple of days later Brer Possum came over to Brer Coon's house for supper.

"How you doing, Brer Coon?"

Brer Coon don't say a word.

"Something the matter?" Brer Possum wondered.

"I don't run with cowards."

"Who you calling a coward?" Brer Possum wanted to know, rolling up his sleeves like he was ready to fight.

"You! I don't want nothing to do with them who lie down on the ground and play dead when there's a fight to be fought."

Brer Possum started laughing. "Have mercy, Brer Coon! You think I did that 'cause I was scared. Why, I wasn't a bit more scared than you are right now. I knew you could whup Brer Dog and I was just laying there watching you do away with him."

Brer Coon wasn't about to buy a lie that sounded that much like a lie.

But Brer Possum insisted. "I tell you I wasn't scared of Brer Dog. When he come running at us, I was getting ready to give him a taste of my right uppercut, when the first thing I know, his nose was in among my ribs. Well, I'm about the most ticklish thing in the world. When his nose touched my ribs, I just fell out like I was dead. That's a fact. Tickling is the one thing in this world I can't stand. Now you put me in a fight where there ain't no tickling and you'll see some fighting!"

And you know something? To this very day, if you want peace from a possum, just touch him in the ribs. He'll fall over like he's dead every time.

The Baby Who Loved Pumpkins

There was a poor woman who had a lot of children. She went down to the creek one day to wash all the clothes.

When she got there she saw an old man sitting on the bank.

"Howdy," he spoke.

She howdied back.

"If it ain't too much trouble, would you mind washing my coat for me?" the old man asked.

The woman said it wouldn't be a bit of trouble. She washed his coat, wrung it real good, and gave it back to him.

The man thanked her. He reached in his pants pocket and pulled out a string of black beads. He gave them to her and said, "When you get home, go behind your house and you will see a pumpkin tree filled with pumpkins. Bury the beads at the root of the tree and then ask for as many pumpkins as you want."

The old man went his way. When the woman finished her washing, she went home and did as the old man had told her. She asked for a pumpkin and a plump pumpkin floated out of the tree and landed at her feet. The woman did not believe her good fortune. She didn't want to be greedy, but for the first time she and her children would have enough to eat.

I know that you think a pumpkin ain't good for nothing except to make a jack-o'-lantern out of at Halloween. Well, you wrong about that. You can make pumpkin fritters and pumpkin bread. You can bake it like squash; you can boil it like turnips. You can toast the seeds and eat them like peanuts. Anybody who knows their way around a kitchen can do a lot with pumpkins, and this woman definitely knew her way around the kitchen! Soon, the woman and her children were healthy and feeling all right about the world.

One morning the woman opened her front door and there, on the doorsill, was a little baby. She looked up and down the road, wondering who had left the baby. She didn't see anyone.

She took the baby and put him with her other children. This was a witch-baby, however, and when the woman served pumpkins to her children, the witch-baby ate all them pumpkins. The woman took the baby and put it back outside.

As soon as she did, the baby turned into a grown man. The man walked down to the creek where he saw an old man sitting on the bank.

"Would you please comb my hair?" the old man asked.

"Comb it yourself!"

"Would you like some pumpkin?" the old man wanted to know.

"Now you talking my kind of talk."

The old man told him where the pumpkin tree was. "But it is very very very important that you only ask for one pumpkin."

The man nodded and went off to the pumpkin tree. When he saw how many pumpkins were in that tree, he hollered, "I want all the pumpkins!"

The pumpkins fell out of the tree and smashed him, knocked him flat, broke his giblets, pounded him into peanut butter and jelly, and killed him dead, which is what he was supposed to be.

Impty-Umpty and the Blacksmith

Back when folks knew a lot more and a lot less than what they know now, a blacksmith had a shop at the big crossroads. I can hear you getting ready to ask me where was the big crossroads? That's a good question, but it has a curious answer.

It seems that when people were going somewhere and coming back from that where, they passed the blacksmith's shop and it didn't matter which way they went and came. That was confusing to the folks who were doing the going and the coming, since they didn't always go and come back the same way. It didn't matter. Somewhere during their going and coming they would hear a whanging and a clanging and would look up and there was the blacksmith's shop, red inside from the fire.

In the wintertime the blacksmith's shop wasn't a bad place to be because the fire going all day kept it quite warm. It was so warm, in fact, that the shop held a lot of the warmth through the night, a fact that Brer Rabbit discovered one cold night.

After the blacksmith went to his quarters in the back of the shop, Brer Rabbit made himself at home by the fire. But one morning he overslept, and the blacksmith caught him.

If the blacksmith didn't want Brer Rabbit enjoying any of his heat, he should've said so. Instead, he threw a hammer at Brer Rabbit. If that hammer had hit him, there wouldn't have been enough left of Brer Rabbit to fill the navel of a gnat. But Brer Rabbit dodged the hammer and got away from there.

He went home to the briar patch and thought about

what he was going to do. He hadn't done no harm to the blacksmith's fire. The blacksmith didn't have to throw the hammer at him.

Along about that time Brer Rabbit saw ol' man Billy Rickerson-Dickerson coming down the road. They passed the time of day and caught up on all the news, and when Mr. Billy Rickerson-Dickerson was about to go, Brer Rabbit said, "Could you do me a favor?"

"Don't see why not."

"When you pass the blacksmith shop, stick your head in the door and say, 'Friend, you'll have company soon,' and go on your way. The next person you meet, tell them to do the same."

Word got around fast. Before long, everybody who passed the blacksmith's shop put their head in the door and said, "Friend, you'll have company soon."

The blacksmith wondered what was happening. What did everybody know that he didn't? The blacksmith got so worried that he couldn't sleep and he stayed up, working with his hammer and anvil. Who was the company and how come nobody would tell him who it was?

One night people were sitting in the shop getting warm and watching the blacksmith work. The flames from the forge made their shadows large against the wall. Every time the blacksmith's hammer hit a piece of iron, the sparks flew up in a red shower. It was natural that people started talking about the Bad Place, and quite naturally, that led them to talking about Impty-Umpty, the one who's in charge down there.

The blacksmith worked and listened to the talk. They said Impty-Umpty walked through the world every day and could turn himself into anything except a hog, a monkey, and a cat. If that was the way it was, one of them might be Impty-Umpty. They looked around like they didn't want to know one another anymore.

The blacksmith finished what he had been working on. It was a big iron box with the sides all welded together, and a top that made a tight lid.

Everybody was admiring the box when the door opened and a tall black man stepped inside and bowed.

"Howdy, folks!"

Everybody looked. They had never seen anybody who looked like him. He was black but he didn't look like a black person. His eyes shone like pieces of glass in the moonlight. He was tall and slim and looked like he was clubfooted and doublejointed.

"I hope that you all will excuse me for coming in so suddenly. I used to be a blacksmith and wanted to see the shop and warm myself by the fire."

He walked over to the forge and held his hands over the live charcoals. The fire sprung up like somebody had poured gasoline on it. The flames burned white, then blue, then green, and got bigger and bigger until they wrapped around the Black Man's hands like snakes.

Nobody said a word.

After a few minutes, the Black Man took his hands out of the fire and looked at the blacksmith. "I hear you expecting company soon."

"Who told you?" the blacksmith wanted to know.

"I saw ol' man Rickerson-Dickerson this morning. He told me. When he did, I told him to sit down in the rocking chair and make himself at home. I left right then to see who this company was that's coming to see you."

The people looked at each other. Ol' man Rickerson-

Dickerson died two days ago and had been buried yesterday.

"Where did you see ol' man Rickerson-Dickerson?" somebody asked the Black Man.

"I saw him coming down the road. He looked like he was cold and I invited him in to warm by my fire."

"Did he warm himself?"

The Black Man laughed until smoke came out of his mouth. "He sho' did!" He laughed again. "He sho' did!" The smoke that came out of his mouth had a sharp odor like the smell when you strike a big wooden match.

When the people heard that laugh, when they saw and smelled the smoke that came out of the Black Man's mouth, they started easing toward the door to get away from there. They had a feeling that the blacksmith's company had come!

Soon nobody was left in the shop but the blacksmith and the Black Man. Oh, and outside Brer Rabbit was peeping in through a crack.

The Black Man said, "I've had my eye on you for a while. I used to be a blacksmith, like I said, and you are going at the thing in the wrong way. You don't need a fire and bellows and all that."

"How am I going to get the iron hot enough if I don't have a fire? How can I make what I need to make if I don't have a hammer and tongs?"

"Watch!" The Black Man picked up a piece of iron, held it close to his mouth and blew on it—once, twice. The iron got hot. It got red-hot. It got so hot, it turned white! He put it on the anvil and hit it—once, twice—and there was the prettiest shovel you have ever seen.

"Who are you?" the blacksmith asked, afraid.

"Folks got a lot of different names for me. I'm not proud.

I respond to all of them—Satan, Old Boy, the Devil."

"Impty-Umpty!"

"That one too."

"Folks say that there're three things you can't do."

"And what might those be?" Impty-Umpty asked.

"Folks say you can't change yourself into a hog, or a monkey, or a cat."

Impty-Umpty grinned, jumped in the air, twisted around like he was a gymnast or an ice skater and when he hit the ground, he was a hog. He grunted and scurried around the shop, snuffling the floor and licking up any crumbs he found. Then he lay on the floor and wallowed around and became a monkey. He ran up the wall and sat on the rafters. Then he dropped to the floor and when he landed, he was a little black cat.

The blacksmith grabbed the cat, shoved it in the iron box he had just finished making, slammed the lid tight and locked it! Then he laughed and laughed.

Brer Rabbit had seen everything. He beat the ground hard with his hind foot. It sounded like a loud drumbeat.

"Who's that?' the blacksmith called out.

"I'm the man you put in the box," Brer Rabbit responded.

The blacksmith laughed. "You can't fool me. Impty-Umpty is in here where I put him at, and he'll be impty-umptied before he's emptied."

"Shake the box, man! Shake the box!" Brer Rabbit answered.

The blacksmith shook the box. He didn't hear anything. He shook it again. Still no sound from inside the box.

The blacksmith scratched his head. He put the box on the floor, unlocked the lid and opened it a crack. He didn't

see anything inside. He raised the lid a little higher and when he did, a big bat flew out of the box, hit him in the face, and flew out the door.

Time passed. The day came, like it comes to everybody, when the blacksmith died. The blacksmith knew there wasn't much chance of him getting into heaven, so he went on down to the Bad Place to see Impty-Umpty. He knocked on the door.

"Who's that?" Impty-Umpty wanted to know.

"Ain't nobody but me."

"If you that blacksmith who locked the cat in the box, you can't come in here." Impty-Umpty hollered to one of his children, "Bring the blacksmith a piece of fire and give it to him. He can go start a hell of his own."

I don't know if the blacksmith did that or not, and I hope I don't find out.

The Angry Woman

Strange things went on in the world back in the old times. Like the time the pot chased the angry woman. This was not one of the kinds of pots folks put on the stove today. Those pots are made out of steel or aluminilium, and they shine and you can see your face in them. Whoever heard of such nonsense? If I want to see my face, I'll go look in the mirror.

The kind of pot I'm talking about are the old-timey pots that were black 'cause they hung in the fireplace. These pots had legs, three little stubby legs, and you could set the pot right in the fireplace if you wanted. After being in the fireplace a while, that pot would get right black. You could tell how good the food was going to be by how black the pot was. The blacker the pot, the better the eating. Food out of a shiny pot might be all right for your stomach but it ain't gon' do nothing for your soul.

Long time ago before shiny pots and stoves with electricity in them, there was a woman who lived in a little house back in the woods near a creek. Now this house might've been in Yallerbammer or Georgy. We know it wasn't in Massachewsits or some foreign place like that.

Some folks say the woman was a black woman. Others say she was white. Everybody says she was nine parts evil and it don't make no never mind about the part what was left over. That's about as close to the truth as we can get in this kind of weather.

From what I heard—and I been keeping both ears wide open—she was a very angry person. She had a bad temper. Neighbors said her tongue was long and loud and mighty well hung.

The woman was married, and her husband tried to get along with her. But she always found something to quarrel about. When he chopped the wood, it was either too long or too short. When he brought home meat, it either had too much fat or not enough. When he wanted breakfast, she cooked supper, and when it was time for supper, she put scrambled eggs on the table. When it came to lowdown meanness, this woman was rank and ripe.

The woman didn't know her husband was a conjure man. A conjure man is the kind of man who says hello to a tree, and the tree knows it better say, "Howdy-do" back. He could turn dandelion fluff back into yellow flowers and compose songs for the birds. So the man was not afraid of his wife.

For a while he tried patience and goodness on her. It didn't work. The man knew he had to do something else.

One day when the woman wasn't home, he spit in the fireplace. Then he made an X mark in the ashes, turned around two times, and shook a gourd-vine flower over the pot in the fireplace. That was that.

Don't come asking me what all that meant. I don't know, and I'm not too sure I want to. There's some things you're better off not knowing and how to conjure folks is definitely one.

Whatever it was the man did, there was peace in the house for a few days. The woman acted halfway nice, at least nice for her. One morning, however, she scared the sugar off the frosted flakes and told the yellow in the eggs to get out of the house. It did. The man knew it was time to try something a little stronger.

When she left the house, he made another X in the ashes and put some thunderwood buds and calamus root in the pot. Then he sat down and waited.

When the woman came back, she was snorting and fuming and carrying on like she had been eating fried nails with red-hot peppers.

She started making supper. She made some dumplings and threw them in the pot. Then she threw in some peas and chili peppers. On top of that she flung a sheep's head. She was making sheep's-head stew. Naw, they don't have that at McDonald's, and it wouldn't sell if they did. But my great-grandaddy's half brother's aunt's third cousin told me that it was some sho' 'nuf good eating.

The man stared at the X he had made in the ashes. After

a while, he smelled the calamus root he had put in the pot. Things were about to start happening.

The sheep's head started bumping against one side of the pot and then the other. Suddenly, the head bumped all the dumplings out. A minute later the peas bounced out and across the floor.

"What's wrong with you?" the woman yelled at the pot. "You been fooling around with me for a long time and I'm sick of it. I'll show you a thing or two!"

The woman hurried toward the door.

"Where you going?" the man asked.

"I'm going where I'm going. That's where I'm going!"

She went to the woodpile to get the axe. She was going to turn that pot into scrap metal. The axe was lying on top of the woodpile and saw her coming.

I reckon I should push the pause button on this story 'cause you want to know how the axe could see her coming. How am I supposed to know something like that? Do I look like an axe? Do I talk like an axe? Since I am not an axe, how am I supposed to know how the axe saw her coming? I don't even know if an axe has one eye, two eyes, or seventy-four eyes. All I know is that the axe saw her coming, and that's what I told you. If you want to worry yourself about *how* it did its seeing, well, you just go right ahead, but I'm going to go on with the story.

Now as I was saying before your loud thinking distracted me, the axe was lying on top of the woodpile and saw the woman coming. The axe didn't want anything to do with her. It dropped down behind the woodpile.

The woman went to get it. The axe climbed back on top and fell down the other side. The woman and the axe kept going back and forth for some time.

Although we don't know how many eyes an axe has, we do know this: It has only one leg. So it was only a matter of time before the woman caught it.

The woman hurried back in the house with the axe, ready to murder that pot.

"You better let that pot alone," the man said. "You'll be sorry if you don't."

"You gon' be sorry if you don't keep your mouth off my business."

"If you don't listen to me, it'll be your last chance to listen to anything."

The woman raised the axe. The pot got up from the fire and headed out the door.

How dare that pot run away from *her*! Out the door she went.

The pot had three legs to the woman's two, but the race was on.

Into the woods and over the hill they went, but it wasn't to grandmama's house. The pot took her up hill and down hill, across the creek this way and back across that way. The pot went so fast and so far that after a while the woman was huffing and puffing and feeling weak.

The pot stopped, came back, and started dancing in a circle around her. Around and around it danced, faster and faster, until, dizzy, the woman fell to the ground.

The pot threw a hot coal of fire at her. I don't know where it got the coal from. I don't know if the fire fell on the woman. I do know she was never seen again. Some say she burned up. Others say she ran away and is now living in Massachewsits, but why would she want to do that?

As for the pot, well, the pot danced and laughed until

it had to hold its sides to keep from busting open. It danced all the way back to the house. Then, it washed its face and scraped the mud off its feet and sat back down in the fireplace.

All the while, the man hadn't moved from his chair. In a few minutes he heard some boiling and bubbling in the pot. He got up and looked in. The sheep's head and the peas and some rice were cooking just as sweetly as you please.

That evening the man had a quiet and peaceful supper.

Brer Rabbit Throws a Party

One time all the animals were sitting around, all of 'em, that is, except Brer Rabbit. And 'cause Brer Rabbit wasn't there, he became the topic of conversation.

The animals started remembering all the things he had done to them. Brer Wolf and Brer Fox had the most memories. These were not the kind of memories the animals wanted to remember or memorize, and by the time they finished remembering, they were upset and out-of-sorts. They agreed that the time had come to take care of Brer Rabbit once and for all.

But how were they going to accomplish this?

They thought with their right brains. Then they thought with their left brains. Finally, they thought they had the perfect plan. They would have a big party. Brer Rabbit wouldn't miss a party if he was dead. When he got there, they would do away with him.

Maybe the plan would've worked. Then, maybe it wouldn't have. We'll never know because Brer Rabbit had been stretched out in the shade of a nearby tree listening all the while. So, after the animals had their plan set, Brer Rabbit sneaked away and doubled around, and the animals looked up to see him coming down the big road—bookity-bookity—galloping like a horse that won the Kentucky Derby.

"Well hello, friends! Howdy! I haven't seen any of you since the last time! Where have you been these odd-come-shorts? If my eyes ain't gon' bad and my breath still smells sweet, that looks like Brer Bear over there with his short tail and sharp teeth. And ain't that Brer Coon down there? My goodness! Looks like everybody is here. Well, that saves me a whole lot of running all over the community to spread the news."

"What news, Brer Rabbit?" the animals asked anxiously.

"Miz Meadows and the girls are going to have a big party tonight and told me to invite everybody. They say they want Brer Bear to do the Roastin' Ear Shuffle. And Brer Coon? They want you to dance the Rack-Back-Davy. I'm gon' play the fiddle, something I haven't done since my oldest child had the mumps and measles on the same day. I took my fiddle down from the shelf this morning. I tuned it up and tightened the bow, and my whole family forgot about breakfast because they were having such a good time dancing to them old-time fiddle tunes I was playing. Miz Meadows say for everybody to put on their Sunday best and she'll see you tonight."

And with that Brer Rabbit went on down the road.

The animals rushed to their homes and spent all afternoon bathing and getting ready for the party.

That night they went over to Miz Meadows's house and knocked on the door.

Miz Meadows come to the door. "My goodness! What are you all doing here? And all dressed up?"

"We come for the party!" they announced.

"Party? I'll party on your heads. You better get out of here before I call the police. How dare you come banging on my door in the middle of the night?"

She slammed the door.

The animals looked at each other very sheepishly and slowly went home.

Brer Rabbit had given them another memory.

Why Brer Fox's Legs Are Black

Now I know you don't know too much about foxes and the like. You probably don't even know that some foxes are red and some are gray, but they all got black legs. How you figure something like that? Well, this is how it came about.

One time Brer Rabbit and Brer Fox was out hunting. Don't ask me what they were hunting for. They could've been hunting lions or tigers. Then again, they might've been hunting for a bargain. Whatever it was, they weren't finding it.

After a while their stomachs started talking, and what their stomachs were saying cannot be put into a book designed for family enjoyment. However, Brer Rabbit had brought along a piece of corn bread to nibble on. Brer Fox hadn't brought anything. Brer Rabbit thought about sharing his corn bread with Brer Fox, but if he did that, then there wouldn't be enough for him. So he walked behind Brer Fox and nibbled on the corn bread whenever his stomach said something that I can't put into a book.

As the day went on, they managed to kill a squirrel or two, but they hadn't brought any matches to make a fire. By now Brer Fox was so hungry that his stomach was talking about him in fourteen different languages. If that wasn't trouble enough, his head was hurting. Plus it was getting late, and the sun was hanging low in the sky and shining red through the trees.

"That's where you can get some fire," Brer Rabbit said.

"Where?"

"Yonder where the sun is. Won't be long before it goes into its hole. As it does, you can get a big chunk of fire

off it. You leave the squirrels here with me and go get the fire. I'd go myself 'cepting you are bigger and more swift and can go faster."

Brer Fox took off to where the sun lived. He trotted; he loped; he galloped; and after a while, he was there. By that time, however, the sun had gone in its hole to get some shut-eye, and Brer Fox couldn't reach down far enough to get a chunk of fire.

"Hey, Mister Sun!" yelled Brer Fox. "Wake up!"

Sun was snoring so loud, he didn't hear a thing.

Brer Fox was determined to get himself a chunk of fire, so he lay down on top of the hole and went to sleep.

The Sun woke up before Brer Fox did. Because the Sun

is the Sun, there is only one thing it can do when it wakes up—and that's to rise.

Sun started climbing out of its hole. Brer Fox was asleep on top of the hole.

In a situation like that, there's got to be a winner and a loser. We don't have to think too long about who was which.

Sun was rising. Brer Fox was asleep. The higher the sun rose, the hotter it got at the top of the hole.

Brer Fox started sweating and moaning in his sleep and woke up just in time to see this ball of fire coming at him. If he hadn't jumped out of the way, he would've gotten burned up. But he didn't jump quite quick enough, because Sun scorched Brer Fox's legs as it went by. And from that day to this, they have been black.

Just goes to show: You got to be careful where you sleep.

How the Witch Was Caught

Sleep is a funny thing. Some nights I go to bed and I'm asleep before my eyes are shut. Other nights I shut my eyes and sleep is on the other side of town. Some nights I sleep a little bit and wake up feeling as if I had slept all night. Other nights I sleep a lot and wake up more tired than if I had stayed up.

When you sleep a lot and wake up tired, it can mean only one thing: A witch was riding you during the night. That's what the ol' folks used to say. Don't ask me why a witch would want to ride somebody. Better than riding the bus, I guess.

I have never seen a witch. At least, not to my knowledge. I have known a few people who I thought might be close relatives, but I myself have never personally sat down face-to-face with a witch and talked about the news of the day. Which don't mean that witches don't exist.

Right here in this town there used to be a man lived down there by the river. He worked hard, saved his money, and bought a house to rent to people so he could make even more money.

But something was the matter with the house he bought. A person would move in in the morning. When they went to bed that night, they felt like they shouldn't go to sleep, because if they did, something told them they wouldn't hear the Sun knock on the door the next morning. They moved out that very same night.

One rainy evening a preacher came along who needed somewhere to stay. He asked around and people told him about the man's empty house.

The preacher went to him.

The man said, "I can't let you stay there. The house is haunted."

"I'd rather stay inside with the ghosts than outside in the rain," the preacher said.

The man took the preacher to the house, made a big fire in the fireplace, and went his way.

The preacher drew a chair up before the fire and waited for the ghosts or the witches, or whatever it was. Nothing came.

After a while the preacher fixed his supper. When he was done eating and was about to wash the dishes, he heard a scratching on the wall.

He looked around. A big black cat was sharpening its

claws on the door. The preacher knew this wasn't a cat you set a bowl of milk out for.

This cat had long white teeth that glistened like stars in the sky on a winter night. It had great big yellow eyes that shone like two moons. And it grinned like it knew something you wished you knew but wouldn't until it was too late.

The cat sidled up to the preacher. Preacher shooed the cat away like it was nothing.

The cat went off.

Preacher wasn't fooled. He washed and dried the dishes. Then he took one of the kitchen knives, sat down by the fire, and waited.

Wasn't long before the black cat came back with twenty black cats just like it, marching behind. They paraded into the room and headed toward the preacher.

The big black cat howled and leaped at the preacher's eyes. The preacher ducked. The cat howled and leaped again. The preacher took a swipe at the cat with the knife and cut off one of its toes.

The cat yowled and ran up the chimney. The other cats followed.

The preacher looked around carefully until he found the cat's toe. He picked it up, wrapped it in a piece of paper, and put it in his pocket. Then he went to bed and slept soundly until Mr. Sun banged on the window the next morning.

Preacher got up, said his prayers, had his breakfast, and prepared to go. He reached in his pocket and felt the piece of paper with the cat's toe in it. The paper felt funny, though. He unwrapped it. Lo and behold, what had been a toe last night was now a finger with a ring on it. The preacher wrapped it up again and put it back in his pocket.

He went to the man's house and thanked him for letting him sleep in the house. "I sure would be obliged to have the opportunity to extend my thanks to your wife and give her my blessing," the preacher finished.

"My wife ain't feeling well this morning, but I'll take you in to her."

The wife lay in bed with the covers pulled up to her chin. Her eyes looked like she hadn't had a wink of sleep.

The preacher held out his hand to the woman. The woman put out her left hand. Preacher took his hand back, like he didn't want to shake her left hand.

"My right hand is crippled," the woman told the preacher.

"Ain't nothing the matter with your right hand that I've ever noticed," her husband put in. "Let me see this hand."

The woman slowly took her right hand from beneath the covers. And guess what? That's right! One of her fingers was missing.

"How did this happen?" the man wanted to know.

"I cut it off," the woman said.

"How did you cut it off?"

"I knocked it off."

"Where did you knock it off?" the man insisted.

"I broke it off."

"When did you break it off?" he said, getting angrier.

The woman got real quiet.

The preacher reached in his pocket, took out the finger, and tried it on the woman's hand. It fit!

"This is the witch what's been haunting your house," the preacher told the man.

The woman yowled like a cat. And right before their eyes, she changed into a big black cat.

The preacher and the man caught the cat and made sure that cat wouldn't haunt anybody's house ever again. After that, the man was able to rent his house, and the folks who lived there were very happy. And so was the man.

———————————

The Man Who Almost Married a Witch

I don't know whether there are witches going around to-day. Seems to me that all the electricity and neon lights and waves from the TVs and radios would make it mighty hard for a witch to know night from day. If I was you, I wouldn't be worried about witches. I'd just enjoy the stories and leave it at that.

Long, long time ago, when the moon was a whole lot bigger than it is now, there was a Witch-Wolf that lived way back in the swamp where the alligators and snakes laid around in the moonshine, flossing each other's teeth.

This Witch-Wolf was about as evil a creature as ever walked the earth without leaving a footprint. When she wasn't making trouble, she was thinking about it, and her thoughts could cause a body misery.

The Witch-Wolf usually took the form of a big black wolf with long claws and green eyes. But when she was hungry she would close her eyes, smack her mouth, and turn into the prettiest woman you ever laid eyes on.

I reckon I got to interrupt the story right here to tell some of you boys who ain't got sense enough to keep your toenails cut short not to go around thinking that every pretty girl might be a witch. That ain't what the story say. The story is about *this* woman and her alone.

The Witch-Wolf's favorite activity was eating men. But before she ate them she would change into a pretty woman, make the man fall in love with her, and marry him. The "I do's" wouldn't be cold before she would shut her eyes, smack her mouth together, and change back into a wolf. Then she'd eat the man up, and that would be that.

One day word got back to her in the swamp that a new

man had moved to town. He had land, but she didn't want the land. He had horses, but she didn't want the horses. He had cows, but she didn't want the cows. She wanted the man.

She closed her eyes, smacked her lips, and there she was, as pretty as a sunrise on a spring morning. Off she went.

The man was sitting on his porch in the cool of the day when a woman walked by, looking as good as a lawn that stays green and never has to be mowed.

"Evening," she said, real sweetlike.

"Good evening to you," he responded, sweating and trembling and grinning all at the same time.

"Mighty nice out this evening, ain't it?"

"It is that."

But before the man could say anything else, the woman walked on down the road, leaving him so eager to see her the next evening that he scarcely slept that night.

Every evening he sat on the porch and waited for her, and every evening she came by. Before long they were sitting on the porch drinking iced tea and talking about the kinds of things men and women talk about.

The woman pretended that she was in love with him. He wasn't pretending about anything. He was sho' 'nuf in love, but something was holding him back. He wanted to ask her to marry him, but the words wouldn't come out of his mouth.

The man was in love but he wasn't dumb. Something about the woman didn't feel right. For one, where did she come from? She wouldn't tell him. Where did she live? She wouldn't tell him. Who were her people? How did she make a living? She wouldn't tell him.

He decided to do some asking around. But who should

he ask? He studied on the situation for a while and finally decided to go see Judge Rabbit. He'd been living in them parts longer than anybody else.

The man went to Judge Rabbit's house and knocked on the door.

"Who's that?" Judge Rabbit called out.

"It's me," answered the man.

"Mighty short name for a grown man," Judge Rabbit said. "Give me the full entitlements."

The man gave out his full name, and Judge Rabbit let him in. They sat down by the fire, and the man started telling Judge Rabbit about the beautiful woman he had met.

"What's her name?" Judge Rabbit asked.

"Mizzle-Mazzle."

Judge Rabbit got very quiet. He made a mark in the ashes in the fireplace. "How old is she?"

The man told him.

Judge Rabbit made another mark. "Has she got eyes like a cat?"

The man thought for a moment. "I guess she does."

Judge Rabbit made another mark in the ashes. "Are her ears kind of pointed at the top?"

The man did some more thinking. "They might be."

Judge Rabbit made yet another mark in the ashes. "Is her hair yellow?"

The man didn't need to worry his mind over that one. "Yes, it is."

Judge Rabbit made another mark. "She got sharp teeth?"

The man nodded.

Judge Rabbit made still another mark and frowned. "I thought Mizzle-Mazzle had moved out of the country. But here she is galloping around, just as natural as a dead pig in the sunshine."

"What're you talking about, Judge?"

"If you want trouble with trouble that doubles and triples trouble, marry Mizzle-Mazzle."

The man looked scared. "What should I do?"

"You got any cows?"

"Plenty."

"Well, here's what you do. Ask Mizzle-Mazzle if she is a good housekeeper. She'll say yes. Ask her if she can cook. She'll say yes to that. Ask her if she can clean pots and pans. She'll say yes. Ask her if she can do the laundry. She'll say yes. Then, ask her if she can milk the red cow. And watch what she says."

The man thanked Judge Rabbit and went home. When he got there, the woman was waiting for him.

"How you doing today?" he asked her.

"Fine. How you?"

"I ain't feeling too good," the man said.

"How come?"

"I'm not rightly sure. It might be because I'm lonely."

"Why are you lonely?"

"I guess it's because I ain't married."

The woman started batting her eyes real fast and running her tongue over her lipstick to make it shine. "What you looking for in a wife?"

"Well, I need somebody who can take care of the house when I'm gone and somebody to keep me company when I'm home. Are you a good housekeeper?"

"Why, yes. I am."

"Can you cook?"

"Why, yes."

"Can you clean pots and pans?"

"Indeed."

"Can you do the laundry?"

"Yes."

"Can you milk the red cow?"

The woman jumped and screamed so loud, the man almost fell over. "You don't think I'd let some cow kick me, do you?"

"The cow is as gentle as a baby."

The woman was still upset, but after a moment she said, "Well, I suppose I could try to milk the cow, if that's what you wanted me to do. But first, let me show you how well I can take care of a house."

Bright and early the next morning the woman came and

cleaned the house from attic to cellar and back again.

The day after that she fixed him the best meal he had ever had. The day after that she cleaned the pots and pans. They shone so much like mirrors that Mr. Sun stayed a little longer at the man's house to look at himself in them.

The day after that she did the laundry and got the whites whiter than white, and the colored clothes stood up and started singing a commercial.

The day following that one, she came to milk the red cow. The man watched from a distance.

She walked into the cow pen with a pail. The cow smelled the witch in her blood. Cow snorted, pawed the ground, and lowered its head like it was going to charge. Before the woman knew it, that's just what the cow did.

The woman leaped the fence, and as she did so, smacked her lips together. She changed into a wolf and disappeared. She hasn't been seen from that time to this.

Why Dogs Are Tame

Back in the days when people and animals lived on the earth like kinfolk, Brer Dog ran with the other animals. He galloped with Brer Fox and loped with Brer Wolf, and cantered with Brer Coon. He went through all the gaits and had as good a time as the other animals and as bad a time too.

It was after one of them bad times that Brer Dog started thinking. Somewhere between Monday morning and Saturday night Brer Dog was sitting in the shade, scratching and thinking about the winter that had just ended. The wind had carried knives and cut through everything standing in its path. Hungriness built a skyscraper in Brer Dog's stomach and moved in with all his kin. Brer Dog was so thin he would've counted his ribs if he had known his numbers. He didn't want to go through another winter like that.

That's what Brer Dog was thinking when Brer Wolf came meandering along.

"Howdy, Brer Dog!"

"Howdy back, Brer Wolf!"

"Brer Dog, you look like you and food are angry at each other. Not that I'm on the friendliest of terms with food myself."

"I hear you," Brer Dog responded.

They commiserated with one another for a while and then Brer Wolf asked, "So what are you up to today?"

"It don't make no difference what I'm up to if I don't find dinner."

"You can't have dinner if you don't have a fire."

"Where am I going to get fire?"

Brer Wolf thought for a minute. "Well, the quickest way I know is to borrow some from Mr. Man and Miz Woman."

"That's a risky proposition."

"I know it."

Mr. Man had a walking cane that he could point at you and blow your lights out.

Brer Dog was desperate, though. "I'll go for the fire," he told Brer Wolf, and off he went.

Before long he was sitting by the gate outside Mr. Man's house. If the gate had been closed, Brer Dog would've gone back from where he came. But some of the children had been playing and left the gate open. Brer Dog didn't want to go through the gate 'cause he didn't want to get his lights blown out. On the other hand, his lights were getting dim because he was so hungry. He walked through the gate as scared as scared can be.

He heard hogs grunting and pigs squealing and hens cackling and roosters crowing, but he didn't turn his head toward grunt or squeal, cackle or crow. He started toward the front door, but it looked too big and white. He went to the back door, and from inside he heard children laughing and playing. For the first time in his life, Brer Dog felt lonely.

He sat down by the back door, afraid to knock. He waited. After a while somebody opened the door and then shut it real quick. Brer Dog didn't see who it was because his eyes were on the ground.

A few minutes later Mr. Man came to the door. In his hand was the stick that would put your lights out. "What you want?" he asked Brer Dog.

Brer Dog was too scared to say anything, so he just wagged his tail.

"As far as I know, you ain't got no business here, so be on your way," Mr. Man said.

Brer Dog crouched down close to the ground and wagged his tail some more. Mr. Man looked at him real hard, trying to decide whether or not to shoot him.

Miz Woman wondered who her husband was talking to. She came to the door and saw Brer Dog crouching on the ground, wagging his tail, his tongue hanging out of the side of his mouth, his eyes so big and wet that he looked like he was going to cry at any minute.

"Poor fella," Miz Woman said. "You not going to hurt anybody, are you?"

"No, ma'am," Brer Dog responded. "I just come to ask if I could borrow a chunk of fire."

"My goodness! What you need a chunk of fire for?" she wanted to know.

"He wants to burn us out of house and home," Mr. Man put in.

"I wouldn't do that," Brer Dog said. "I need the fire so that if I get something to eat, I can cook it. And if I don't get nothing to eat, at least I'll be able to keep warm on these chilly nights."

"You poor thing. Why don't you come in here to the kitchen and get as warm as you want."

"I don't want that animal in my house," Mr. Man protested.

"He's so cuuuuute," Miz Woman said.

Brer Dog didn't say anything. He just tried to look cute as he trotted in the house.

There was a big fireplace in the kitchen, and he sat down on the hearth. The children were sitting around the table eating their supper. After a while, Brer Dog was feeling right splimmy-splammy.

But he was still very hungry. He looked up with his big eyes and saw the children eating corn bread and collard greens and ham hocks. His eyes followed the children's hands from plate to mouth, mouth to plate, plate to mouth, mouth to plate.

Miz Woman saw Brer Dog watching the children. She went to the cabinet and got a plate and put some ham, corn bread, and juice from the greens on it and set it down in front of Brer Dog.

Brer Dog gobbled it up with one gulp. It wasn't enough to satisfy his hunger, but he was afraid that if they saw how hungry he really was, they wouldn't let him stay.

So he stretched out in front of the fire, yawned loudly, and put his head across his paws and pretended he had fallen asleep.

Wasn't long before he smelled a familiar smell. He smelled the familiar smell of Brer Wolf. He raised his head and looked toward the door.

Mr. Man noticed the dog looking toward the door. "Is there something sneaking around out there?"

Brer Dog got up, trotted to the door, and growled a low growl.

"There's a varmint out there, ain't it?" Mr. Man said, getting his rifle from over the fireplace. He opened the door, and what should he see but Brer Wolf running out the gate. Mr. Man raised the rifle and—*kerblam!* Brer Wolf howled. The shot missed Brer Wolf, but the scare was a bull's-eye.

After that Mr. Man had a new appreciation for Brer Dog. Brer Dog showed he could be useful in many ways. He headed the cows off when they made a break to go into the woods. He took care of the sheep. Late up in the night, he warned Mr. Man if any varmints were lurking around. When Mr. Man went hunting, Brer Dog was there to keep him company. And he played with Mr. Man's and Miz Woman's children as if he was one of them. And for all that, Brer Dog didn't want anything more than food to eat and a place in front of the fire.

Before long Brer Dog was fat and sleek. One day he was out by himself in the woods when he met up with Brer Wolf.

"Howdy, Brer Wolf."

Brer Wolf don't say nothing for a while. Finally, "So why didn't you come back with the fire that day?"

Brer Dog pointed to the collar around his neck. "See this? I belong to Mr. Man and Miz Woman now."

"You look like you haven't missed a meal in a long time. How come I can't come there and have them own me?"

"Come on!"

The next morning Brer Wolf knocked on Mr. Man's door. Mr. Man looked out to see who it was. When he saw Brer Wolf, Mr. Man got his rifle and went to the door.

Brer Wolf tried to be as polite as he could. He smiled. I don't know if you've ever seen a wolf smile. It is not a pleasant sight. Mr. Man saw a mouth full of teeth as sharp as grief. Mr. Man raised his rifle and—*kerblam!*—took a shot at Brer Wolf.

Some folks say he missed. Others say he gave him natural air-conditioning. I don't know how that part turned

out. What I do know is that Brer Dog has been living in people's houses ever since.

How Tinktum Tidy Recruited an Army for the King

This is a story about a short, ugly man. That's the first indication that this is not a fairy tale. In fairy tales the man is always a tall and handsome prince. But there are a lot more short and ugly people in the world than tall, handsome ones. Why, then, are all the fairy tales about somebody who there ain't many of?

Well, the man in this story may have been short and ugly, but he was as smart as he was ugly, which means that he was *very* smart. He was also prosperous and owned hundreds of acres of land.

His name was Linktum Lidy Lody. That was his given name. His family name was Tinktum Tidy. Other folks called him Linktum Tidlum Tidy. One or two called him Tinktum Tidlum. But me, I call him Tinktum Tidy and Linktum Lidy Lody Tinktum Tidy, so that's who he'll be.

When it came to brains, Tinktum Tidy had enough for two people. Everybody knew it, and whenever they had a problem, they'd bring it to him and he would solve it for them.

Word eventually reached the king that Tinktum Tidy was the smartest man in the kingdom. The Lord had not been kind to the king in the brain department. Didn't make any difference. You don't have to be smart to be king or president. (I could name presidents who didn't have *any* brains.) You just have to know who the smart people are and get them to work for you. So, that's what the king did. He sent word that he wanted to meet Tinktum Tidy.

Tinktum Tidy set out for where the king lived. When he got there, he told the royal guards that the king had sent for him. They took him into a big room where there were many other people.

Everybody looked at Tinktum Tidy 'cause he was so short and ugly. Tinktum Tidy looked back at them like they were crazy.

The king came in and sat down on his throne. He looked at everybody, and his eyes stopped at Tinktum Tidy. "You the shortest and the ugliest thing I've ever seen. What do you want?"

"I'm Linktum Lidy Lody Tinktum Tidy."

"So what?"

"You sent for me."

"I did?" The king was confused. "Why did I send for you?"

"How should I know?"

One of the king's counselors whispered for a long time in the king's ear.

"Now I remember," said the king. "I understand you got more brains than anybody in the kingdom." The king reached in his pocket and took out eleven grains of corn. "If you're so smart, take these eleven grains of corn and bring me back eleven strong men to put in my army."

Tinktum Tidy took the corn, tied it in his handkerchief, bowed, and went his way.

All that day he traveled. When night came, he stopped at an inn, which is what they called hotels and motels back in that time.

"What's your name and where you from and where might you be going?" the innkeeper wanted to know.

"I'm Linktum Lidy Lody Tinktum Tidy. I'm from Chuckerluckertown, and I'm on a long journey."

The innkeeper showed Tinktum to his room. Tinktum Tidy heard a loud squawking noise. "What's that?"

"That ain't nothing but Molly the Goose."

Tinktum Tidy took out the handkerchief and untied it. "Here are eleven grains of corn the king gave me. I'm afraid Molly the Goose will come in here and eat them."

The man said, "Don't you worry none about that. I'll make sure all the doors are shut tight."

Way up in the night when everybody was sleep, Tinktum Tidy took the corn and dropped it through a crack in the floor.

The next morning, when everybody was waking up, they heard Tinktum Tidy yelling and screaming, "I told you so! I told you so! Molly the Goose has eaten the king's corn! Molly the Goose has eaten the king's corn!"

When the innkeeper heard that, he got scared. He grabbed Molly the Goose and gave her to Tinktum Tidy. "Here! You can have the goose! Now, get away from here before the king comes looking for his corn."

Tinktum Tidy took the goose and went on down the big road. He traveled all day, and close to nightfall he came to another inn.

When it came time to retire for the night, Tinktum Tidy tied Molly the Goose to the bed and called the innkeeper.

"My name is Linktum Lidy Lody Tinktum Tidy. This here is Molly the Goose. She ate the eleven grains of corn the king gave me." Just then a noise came from outside. "What's that?" Tinktum Tidy wanted to know.

"That's nothing but Boo-Boo Black Sheep."

"I'm afraid Boo-Boo Black Sheep will come in here during the night and eat Molly the Goose, who ate the king's eleven grains of corn."

The innkeeper said, "Don't worry. I'll make sure all the doors are locked tight."

In the middle of the night when it was hard to tell the sleeping from the dead, Tinktum Tidy broke Molly the Goose's neck. Then he sneaked outside and threw her body in the barnyard next to Boo-Boo Black Sheep.

The next morning, when everybody was starting to wake up, they heard Tinktum Tidy hollering and yelling, "I told you so! I told you so! Boo-Boo Black Sheep killed Molly the Goose, who ate the eleven grains of corn the king gave me. The king is going to be very angry at somebody."

The innkeeper got scared 'cause the king's corn was inside the goose, and the goose was now dead, and the king might blame the innkeeper. He gave Boo-Boo Black Sheep to Tinktum Tidy. "Here! Take the sheep and get away from here. You brought me bad luck!"

Tinktum Tidy took Boo-Boo Black Sheep and went on down the big road. He traveled all day until he came to another town and in that town was an inn.

When bedtime came he tied Boo-Boo Black Sheep to his bed and called for the innkeeper. "I see you have a cow. What's your cow's name?"

The innkeeper said, "That's Brindle Cow."

"Well, this is Boo-Boo Black Sheep, who killed Molly the Goose, who ate the eleven grains of corn the king gave me. I'm afraid Brindle Cow will kill Boo-Boo Black Sheep."

"I'll make sure all the doors are locked tight."

Sometime between moondown and sunup, Tinktum Tidy

killed Boo-Boo Black Sheep and put him in the pen with Brindle Cow.

The next morning, about the time folks started yawning themselves awake, they heard Tinktum Tidy hollering and yelling, "I told you so! I told you so! Brindle Cow done killed Boo-Boo Black Sheep, who killed Molly the Goose, who ate the eleven grains of corn the king gave me."

The man heard the king's name and got scared. "Here! Take the cow! Get on away from here before you bring me more bad luck."

Tinktum Tidy took Brindle Cow and went off down the big road. He walked all that day until he came to the next town and got a room for the night at the inn.

He said to the innkeeper, "I noticed you got a horse tied up outside. Well, this here is Brindle Cow, that killed Boo-Boo Black Sheep, that ate Molly the Goose, who ate the eleven grains of corn the king gave me. I'm afraid your horse is going to kill Brindle Cow."

"Whoever heard of a horse killing a cow?"

The innkeeper should not have said that. Way up in the night, Tinktum Tidy killed Brindle Cow and put the carcass in the pen with the horse.

Next morning Tinktum Tidy woke everybody up hollering and yelling, "I told you so! I told you so! The horse killed Brindle Cow, that killed Boo-Boo Black Sheep, that ate Molly the Goose, who ate the eleven grains of corn the king gave me."

The mention of the king's name scared the innkeeper. "Here! Take the horse and go on about your business!"

Tinktum Tidy got on the horse and went trotting down the big road. He rode and he rode until he came to a creek. Sitting between the road and the creek was an old man. Linktum Lidy Lody Tinktum Tidy stopped and looked at the old man. The old man looked at Linktum Lidy Lody Tinktum Tidy.

"How do?" the old man said.

"How do?" Tinktum Tidy returned.

"Some dust blowed in my eyes, son. Would you wipe my eyes for me?" the old man requested.

Tinktum Tidy got off the horse and wiped the old man's eyes.

"Thank you," the old man said.

"You're welcome," Tinktum Tidy responded. Then he got back on the horse and prepared to go his way.

"Come scratch my head," the old man said.

Tinktum Tidy got off the horse and scratched the old man's head.

"Thank you, son. Thank you."

"You're mighty welcome." Tinktum Tidy got on his horse and prepared to ride away.

"Come help me get up," the old man said.

Tinktum Tidy got off the horse and helped the old man up. A strange thing happened. As the old man began to get up, youth and strength came back into his body. By the time he was standing erect, he looked like a young man.

"Son, I been sitting here for almost ten years. You're the first person who ever did what I asked. Some laughed at me. Some cursed me, and all went by. But it's a funny thing. Everyone that passed me was set on by the eleven robbers who live just down the road. The robbers took all their money and clothes and kicked them back out in the world. Now, seeing as how you did what I asked you, I'll be more than pleased to do what you ask."

Tinktum Tidy told the man that he had to get eleven strong men for the king's army.

The man said, "Well, them eleven robbers are strong enough to be in the army. Here's what you do. Keep on down the big road until you come to a big white house. Ride around the house seven times to the right and seven times to the left and say whatever words come into your head."

Tinktum Tidy went down the big road and came to the big white house. He rode around it seven times to the right and seven times to the left. "This is the horse that killed the Brindle Cow, that killed Boo-Boo Black Sheep, that ate Molly Goose, that ate the eleven grains of corn the king gave me. I want eleven strong men for the king's army."

The front door of the white house opened and the eleven robbers came marching out. They got on their horses and Tinktum Tidy led them right to the king.

After that Linktum Lidy Lody Tinktum Tidy didn't look so short to people, and Linktum Lidy Lody Tinktum Tidy didn't look so ugly either.

Why Guinea Fowls Are Speckled

This story is about the guinea fowls. A guinea fowl is a bird of the pheasant family. It come from Africa, which is why it's called a guinea, 'cause it's from Guinea. It's about the size of a pheasant, which is about the size of a turkey. Its feathers are kind of blue-black, with white spots all over.

But that ain't how it always was. The guinea used to be

spotless. This story is about how come they aren't that way now.

One day Sister Cow was grazing in the field with her calf. After a while along came a drove of Guineas.

"Howdy, Sister Cow!"

"Howdy!"

The Guineas pecked around in the ground while exchanging the news of the neighborhood with Sister Cow. Suddenly, they heard a curious noise from the other side of the field. The Guineas looked around but didn't see anything. Sister Cow looked around. She didn't see anything either.

The Guineas went back to pecking and Sister Cow went back to chewing her cud. Before long the noise came again, only this time it was closer. The Guineas and Sister Cow looked up. Standing between them and sundown was a great big Lion!

The Lion loved cow meat more than anything in creation. He shook his hairy head, roared a hairy roar, pawed the ground a couple of times, and made a rush for Sister Cow.

The Guineas ran this way and that, and they ran around and around. However, Sister Cow stood her ground. When the Lion charged, Sister Cow dropped her head, pointed her horns toward him, and pawed the earth.

The Lion stopped and began circling slowly around the Cow. Every way the Lion went, Sister Cow turned, keeping her horns always pointed at the Lion.

The Guineas were watching all this. They saw that Sister Cow wasn't afraid, and this gave them heart. Next thing you know one of the Guineas ran out between Sister Cow and the Lion, turned her back to the Lion, and began scratching and kicking up dirt and grass in the Lion's face.

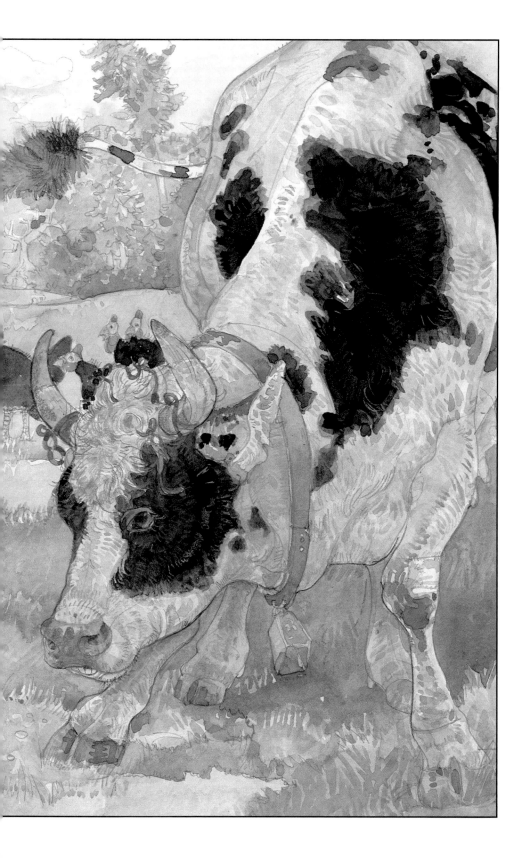

When that Guinea had had enough fun, she ran back to the group and another Guinea ran out and had her some fun kicking up dirt and grass on the Lion.

Before you know it, the Lion had so much dust and dirt and grass in his eyes that he couldn't see his hand in front of his face. He was growling and roaring and snapping at the air, and he got so mad that he made a blind plunge at Sister Cow.

Sister Cow dipped her head and caught the Lion on her horns. That was the end of the Lion.

Sister Cow called the Guineas to her. "I want to thank you for all your help."

"Don't concern yourself with us, Sister Cow. You had your fun and we had ours."

"That's true, but I would like to show you my gratitude. What can I do for you?"

The Guineas conferred among themselves for a while, then one said, "What we need doing for us, you can't do it. But I wish you could."

"And what might you need?"

"We need to be fixed so that we can't be seen from far away. We look blue in the sun, and we look blue in the shade, which makes it hard for us to hide."

Sister Cow chewed her cud and thought. "Somebody get me a pail," she said finally.

"What you want with a pail?" one of the Guineas asked.

"Get it. You'll see."

When the Guinea came back with the pail, Sister Cow stood over it and let down milk until the pail was full. Then she told the Guineas to get in a row. They lined up. Sister Cow dipped her tail in the milk, and sprinkled each Guinea, and as she did so, she said, "I loves this one." Then she would sing:

Oh, Blue, go away! You shall not stay!
Oh, Guinea, be Gray, be Gray!

She sprinkled all the Guinea hens. When she finished they sat in the sun until they dried. That's why until this day, guinea hens are speckled.

Why the Guineas Stay Awake

Every night when it came time for the Guineas to go to bed, they were asleep the minute their heads hit the pillows. Don't come asking me what kind of pillows they had. I suspect they were feather pillows, however.

One night Brer Fox decided to be sociable and visit with the Guineas after they had gone to sleep.

Along toward the shank of the evening, and if you look carefully on the clock you'll find the shank between midnight and 3:00 A.M., Brer Fox arrived at where the Guineas were sleep. Some folks when they go somewhere to be sociable would turn around and go back home if they found everybody asleep. Brer Fox was not that kind of man.

Brer Fox looked at the Guineas. They looked so fine and so fat, Brer Fox felt like they were kinfolk. "I believe I'll just shake hands with one and then I'll go."

That's what Brer Fox did, but something happened. When he grabbed a Guinea hen, his grip must have been too tight, because when he tipped his hat and left, the Guinea hen went with him.

You should've heard the racket the Guineas made when

they discovered that Brer Fox had made off with one of them. They squalled and squalled until they woke up the whole neighborhood. The dogs were barking, the owls were hooting, the horses were whinnying, the cows were mooing, the chickens were clucking and crowing, and all the people were yelling, "SHUT UP!"

The next night the Guineas were so scared that they refused to shut their eyes. And from that night to this, Guineas don't sleep at night. I don't know when they do sleep. I reckon they nod off during the day, but I don't know anybody who has ever seen them. I do know this, though: Guinea hens stay awake all night. I hope the one Brer Fox took was good eating, 'cause that was the last one he ever ate.

Brer Fox and the White Grapes

One day Brer Rabbit was going through the woods. Don't come asking me where he was going because I don't know. Brer Rabbit probably didn't know where he was going. If *he* didn't know where he was going, I cannot be expected to know what he didn't know. And, no, I don't know where he was coming from either.

I do know that while he was going through the woods he happened to run into Brer Fox.

"How you, Brer Fox?"

Brer Fox shook his head. "I ain't."

"What's the problem?"

"I'm hungry, Brer Rabbit."

"I'm glad I'm me and not you."

"Why so?"

" 'Cause my stomach is full of white grapes," Brer Rabbit told him.

"White grapes!" Brer Fox started to dribble at the mouth. "Brer Rabbit, where did you find white grapes, and how come I didn't find them?"

"Well, I don't know why you didn't find them, Brer Fox. Seems that some folks see straight. Some folks see crooked. Some folks see in curves, and some folks see around corners. And then some folks have their eyes open and don't see a thing. Me, I saw the white grapes and I ate every last one of them."

"Don't tell me that, Brer Rabbit," moaned Brer Fox.

"Well, I ate all the white grapes growing off the vine covering this one particular tree. There're probably white grapes growing off the vines on other trees in the same vicinity."

"Well, don't just stand there, Brer Rabbit. Let's go. Show me where this vicinity is."

Brer Rabbit shook his head. "I don't know, Brer Fox. You want to get me way out there deep in the woods by myself where nobody could hear me holler if I had to. Once you get me out there, you'll try and do away with me."

Brer Fox was hurt. "Brer Rabbit, I ain't got no such a thing in mind. What kind of person do you think I am? I will tell you what kind of a person I am, Brer Rabbit. I am a hungry person. That is who I am."

Brer Rabbit looked like he still wasn't sure. "Brer Fox, you have played so many tricks on people, I'd be a fool to go way off in the woods with you."

The conversation went back and forth until Brer Fox promised Brer Rabbit that he wouldn't play any tricks on him or try to do away with him. If Brer Fox had the sense he was born with he would've gotten Brer Rabbit to promise the same thing.

Off they went until they came to a big tree covered with grape vines. The grapes were not ripe, however, which Brer Rabbit knew and Brer Fox would've known if he would've seen what his eyes were looking at. But all he could see was his hunger. When a man looks at the world through hungry eyes, everything looks good to eat.

Brer Fox looked up at the tree. "How am I going to get the grapes?"

"Do like I did."

"How did you did?"

"I climbed for them."

"Climb? How am I going to do that?" Brer Fox wanted to know.

"Grab with your hands, climb with your legs, and I'll push your bottom."

So, Brer Fox grabbed and climbed and Brer Rabbit pushed. Soon, Brer Fox was high enough to grab the lowest limb. From there he made it on his own until he was high enough to eat the grapes. He shoved some in his mouth.

"Ow!" he hollered. "These grapes are bitter!" He spit them out.

"Well, they *looked* ripe," said Brer Rabbit. "I guess you better come on down, Brer Fox, and we'll go hunt for another tree."

Brer Fox started down the tree. He was doing fine until he got to the lowest limb. It was a long way from there to the ground. What was he going to do? He didn't have

any claws to cling by and not enough leg to do any serious clamping.

"Come on down, Brer Fox! Come on down!" Brer Rabbit yelled.

"How am I supposed to do that?"

"I'll tell you what, Brer Fox. Jump, and I'll catch you." Brer Rabbit stood out from the tree with his arms out. "I'm ready, Brer Fox!"

Brer Fox looked up. He looked down. He looked all around.

"Come on, Brer Fox! My arms are getting tired!"

Brer Fox took a deep breath, closed his eyes and jumped.

The instant he jumped, Brer Rabbit hopped out the way, crying, "Ow! Ow! Ow! I got a thorn stuck in my foot! Ow! It hurts!"

It didn't hurt half as bad as Brer Fox hurt when he hit the ground! KERBLAMABLAM BLAM BLAM! It took Brer Fox a while to pick himself up and feel all around to make sure he still had all his parts and they were in working order.

As for Brer Rabbit, he laughed so much, that laughter got fat.

Why the Hawk Likes to Eat Chickens

One of the most awesome sights in nature is a hawk diving from the belly button of the sky and catching something to eat. It's not a sight you see often. You got to be at the right place at the right time and looking in the right direction, 'cause it happens faster than a flea can blink.

Just as Brer Fox was having a problem keeping his belly full, there was a day when Brer Hawk was having the same problem. He flew this way. He flew that way. He even flew the other way. There was nothing to eat in any direction.

Finally he noticed the Sun up in the elements, and he flew up to see him. "Howdy."

The Sun howdied back, and the two got to talking about first one thing and another the way folks do when they are striking up an acquaintance.

Finally, Brer Hawk told the Sun the troubles he was having finding something to eat.

"Well," offered the Sun, "if you can catch me in bed, I'll show you where to find all you can eat."

Brer Hawk was up bright and early the next morning, but the Sun was already strutting across the sky. Every morning Brer Hawk got up earlier and earlier but he was never early enough. He sat up all night and still the Sun managed to get out of bed before Brer Hawk could catch him.

Not only was Brer Hawk losing sleep, he was also getting skinnier and skinnier. One morning after he had failed to catch the Sun in bed again, he was sitting in the top of a great big pine tree, wondering what to do. Just then he heard something on the ground calling him.

"Yo! Brer Hawk!"

He looked down and saw Brer Rooster. "What you want?" Brer Hawk hollered. "Stop bothering me. Go scratch up your little worms and cackle over them, but leave me alone."

"What's the matter, Brer Hawk? You in a mighty bad mood. And how come you look so pale? How come you look so lonesome?"

Brer Hawk didn't know if Brer Rooster had a degree in psychotherapy but he sure knew how to ask the right questions and that was good enough. He dropped out of the tree and settled on the fence rail where he could talk to Brer Rooster.

Brer Hawk told him that he had been trying to catch the Sun in bed.

Brer Rooster laughed so hard he almost lost his cock-a-doodle-do. When he managed to stop, he said, "Brer Hawk, why didn't you come to me? I catch the Sun in bed every morning. I'm his alarm clock!"

"You are!"

"I are!"

"Well, I'll be!"

"You'll be what?"

"Never mind," Brer Hawk said.

"If you say so. Tell you what. Sleep here tonight. In the morning when I'm ready to wake the Sun up, you can fly off and catch him in bed."

And that's what happened. The next morning along about three-ninety-seven, Brer Rooster woke up Brer Hawk. "Go get him!"

Brer Hawk stretched his great wings and he was off. Ain't nothing in creation can fly like a hawk. He flew straight up until he passed the morning star. Then he took a left and a right, did a loop-de-loop, and went through the black of night, and there on the other side was where the Sun lived. (The Sun had decided that living in a hole was dangerous after Brer Fox had fallen asleep on top of it.) Brer Hawk walked through the door, past the living room, and right into the bedroom.

There, lying in bed, the covers pulled up to his chin, snoring, was none other than the Sun.

"Time for daybreak!" hollered Brer Hawk. "What you doing laying in bed, you lazy scoundrel. Folks are waiting to eat breakfast and you gon' make 'em late."

"Who that?" the Sun said.

"Me!"

"What you want to wake me up for? Now I'm going to have a headache all day."

"Tough. I'm hungry and you said that if I caught you in bed, you would show me where to find food."

The Sun was mad at having been woken up early. "Who told you where to find me?"

"Brer Rooster."

The Sun raised up from the bed and gave Brer Hawk a big wink with his right eye. "Brer Rooster knows where you can find a meal."

Brer Hawk flew back down to earth and told Brer Rooster what the Sun had said.

"Why would he say something like that? I'm having trouble finding enough food to take care of my own family."

Brer Hawk was desperate now. "Brer Rooster, I'm hungrier than your family. I have got to find something to eat."

"You're welcome to dig here in the dirt with me. The worms are big and juicy this time of year."

Brer Hawk shook his head. He needed a lot more than worms. He flew to the top of the pine tree and sat there wondering what he was going to do.

He hadn't been there long before Miss Hen with all of the children came to help Brer Rooster hunt for worms. That was when Brer Hawk understood why the Sun had winked and sent him back to Brer Rooster.

Brer Hawk dropped out of that tree like bad news. Before anyone knew what was happening, he had grabbed one of the little chickens in his sharp talons and flown away with it.

From that day to this, the Hawk has never been hungry. And from that day to this, Brer Rooster has never told anyone else where the Sun sleeps. It just so happens that I know too, but I think it best if I keep my mouth shut.

The Little Boy and His Dogs

Once upon a time there was a woman who lived in a house beside a road. She had a little boy who, seems to me, was about your size. He might've been a little broader across the shoulders and a little longer in the leg, but if you looked up one side and down the other, he was just about your size. And like you, he was also very smart.

This little boy had a sister. But one day someone came along and kidnapped her. Quite naturally this made the mother and the little boy very sad.

Every day the little boy climbed to the top of the tallest tree and looked in every direction for some sign of his sister. She had vanished without a trace.

One day when he was at the top of the tree, he saw two finely dressed women walking down the road. He hurried and told his mother.

"How are they dressed, Son?"

"Mighty fine, Momma. Mighty fine with puffed out dresses and long green veils."

"How do they look, Son?"

"Like they brand-new, Momma."

"Well, they don't sound like none of our kinfolk, do they, Son?"

"No, they don't, Momma."

The finely dressed ladies came down the road and stopped at the house where the woman and the little boy lived.

"Could we trouble you for some water?" they asked.

The little boy got the dipper and filled it with water. The ladies put the dipper under their veils and drank and drank and drank like they hadn't had water since Adam was a baby.

The little boy said, "Momma? They lapping up the water like animals."

"I reckon that's the way rich folks drink," she responded.

Then the ladies asked for some bread. The little boy got some from the kitchen. The women ate the bread like they hadn't put anything in their stomachs since Eve was in diapers.

"Momma? The women got big long teeth that curve and sparkle in the light."

"I reckon that's how rich people's teeth are, Son."

Then the ladies asked for water to wash their hands. The boy brought the wash basin and filled it with water.

He watched them wash their hands. "Momma? The ladies got hairy hands and arms."

"I reckon that's how rich folks' hands and arms are, Son."

Then the ladies asked the woman if the little boy could show them where the road forked.

The little boy didn't want to go. "Momma, don't nobody need to be shown where the road forks."

"I reckon rich folks ain't got much sense, Son."

The little boy started to sniff and cry because he did not want to go with the two women. His mother told him that he should be ashamed of himself. "Go show the ladies what they want, Son. And who knows? You might find your sister."

The little boy had two dogs. They were bad dogs too. One was named Minnyminny Morack. The other was named Follamalinska. They were so bad that they had to be tied up day and night with great strong ropes.

The little boy got a pan of water and put it in the middle of the floor. Then he got a limb from a willow tree.

"Momma? If the water in the dish turns to blood, let Minnyminny Morack and Follamalinska loose. If the limb from the willow tree starts shaking, set the dogs on my track."

The little boy took some eggs and put them in his pocket in case he got hungry. Then he set off to show the two ladies where the big road forked.

He hadn't gone far before he noticed the two ladies panting like wild animals. He guessed that was how rich folks breathed when the weather was hot and they were tired.

When the ladies thought the little boy wasn't paying them any attention (but he was), one of them dropped down on all fours, just like a wolf. A minute later the other lady dropped down on all fours and started running.

The little boy thought to himself, Well, if that's how rich folks rest themselves when they tired, I better be thinking about resting myself.

He saw a big pine tree and climbed up it quickly.

The animals turned back into ladies and one of them hollered, "What're you doing, little boy?"

"I'm resting myself."

"Why don't you rest on the ground?"

"I can rest better up where it's cool."

The ladies walked around and around the tree. "Little boy, little boy! You better come down and show us how to get to the fork in the big road."

"It's easy, ladies. Keep going straight until the road forks. You can't miss it. And anyway, I'm afraid to come down. What if I fall and hurt one of you?"

"You better come down or we'll tell your mother how bad you are."

The little boy answered, "While you're telling her that, tell her how scared I am."

The ladies were angry now. They growled and snorted. They pulled off their bonnets and their veils and their dresses, and lo and behold, guess what the little boy saw? Two great big panthers! They had great big yellow eyes and long sharp teeth and great long tails. They looked up at the little boy and growled. The little boy shivered. The panthers tried to climb the tree but they had clipped their claws so they could wear gloves, which meant they couldn't climb anymore.

Then one of the panthers sat down in the road and made some marks in the sand.

BOING! The tails of both panthers turned into axes. One panther was on one side of the tree; the other panther was on the other side, and they started axing away. Before long, the tree was ready to fall.

The little boy remembered the eggs in his pocket. He took one, broke it, and said, "Place, fill up!"

The places where the panthers had cut the tree filled right up. The tree looked like nothing had ever happened to it.

That didn't bother the panthers. They started whaling away at the tree again. When the tree was almost ready to fall, the boy broke another egg and said, "Place, fill up!" The tree became like new again.

The little boy had only one egg left, and the panthers were once again axing the tree.

Just about this time the little boy's mother noticed the pan of water turning to blood. She went to the yard and untied Minnyminny Morack and Follamalinska. As soon as she returned to the house she saw the willow limb trembling and shaking. She hollered to the dogs, "Go!" The dogs took off!

The little boy heard the dogs coming. "Come on, my dogs! Come on!"

The panthers stopped axing and listened. "You hear anything?" one asked the other.

"I don't hear nothing," said the little boy. "Go on with your chopping."

The panthers went back to axing, but they couldn't shake the feeling that dogs were coming. Before they could change from panthers to ladies, Minnyminny Morack and Follamalinska caught them.

The little boy hollered to the dogs, "Shake 'em and bite 'em. Drag 'em round and round until you drag 'em ten miles."

So the dogs drug the panthers ten miles. By the time they drug them back, those panthers were cold and stiff.

The little boy climbed down from the tree and decided to see if he couldn't find his sister. Off into the woods he and the dogs went.

They hadn't gone far before he saw a house sitting off by itself. The dogs smelled around the house. The hair on their bodies stood straight up. The boy saw a little girl carrying wood and water. She was very pretty, but she was clothed in rags and crying. Minnyminny Morack and Follamalinska were wagging their tails. The little boy had found his sister.

He went up to her and asked her her name.

"I don't know," she said. She had been scared for so long that she had forgotten.

"Why are your crying?" he wanted to know.

"Because I have to work so hard."

"Whose house is this?"

"It belongs to a huge black Bear. He's the one who makes me work so hard. The water is for the big pot. The wood is to make the water boil, and the boiling water in the pot is how the Bear cooks the people he feeds to his children."

The little boy didn't tell her he was her brother. Instead he said, "Well, I believe I'll stay and have supper with the Bear."

"Oh, no! You mustn't! You mustn't!"

But the little boy walked in the house. He saw that the Bear had two big children. One was sitting on the bed. The other was sitting by the fireplace. The little boy sat down and waited.

The Bear was a long time in coming home, though. So, the little girl cooked supper for herself and the boy. After they ate, the little boy told her that he would love to comb her hair. Her hair hadn't been combed in so long, however, that it was all tangled up. She started crying at the thought of a comb going through it.

"Don't worry," he told her. "I'll be very gentle." He warmed water on the stove, worked it into her hair and combed it until it was soft and curly.

Finally, the Bear came home. He was surprised to see

the little boy sitting there. He was very polite, though, shook the little boy's hand, and admired how pretty the little girl's hair was.

"How did you make her hair look so nice?" the Bear wanted to know.

"It's easy," said the little boy.

"Well, if that's the case, would you mind curling my hair?"

"Why, not at all. Fill the big pot with water."

The Bear filled the big pot with water.

"Build up the fire under the pot and heat the water."

The Bear built up the fire.

"When the water is scalding hot, stick your head in. And your hair will curl right up."

When the water was scalding hot, the Bear stuck his head in. The scalding water curled his hair until it came right off. That was the end of the Bear.

The Bear's children were upset when they saw what happened to their daddy. They started biting the little boy and the little girl. Minnyminny Morack and Follamalinska got hold of them bear children and when the dogs were finished, there wasn't enough left to figure out who they used to be.

Then, the little boy told the little girl he was her brother and they went home to their mother.

The Man and the Wild Cattle

Once there was a man who lived next to a great woods. I don't believe there're any woods in the world big as that woods was. If you got on a horse and rode in a straight line for seven days and seven nights, that's how wide the woods were. If you got on the same horse and made him go as fast as he could go for eleven days and eleven nights, you would go as far as the woods was long.

In these woods were herds of horned cattle. Might've been some deer and moose and other creatures in there, but most of the creatures were horned cattle.

The man would hunt the cattle for their hides. He had

a bow and arrow and two big dogs. What cattle he couldn't get with his bow and arrow, the dogs would get. These dogs were almost as big as the cattle, and they were as ferocious as lion's breath. One dog was named Minny-minny Morack and the other was called Follamalinska.

That's right. The man in this story is the little boy in the last story, after he grew up.

The man and the dogs hunted the horned cattle day and night. Things finally got so bad for the cattle that they had a meeting. They conferred and debated and caucused. Finally they concluded that the only way they had a chance was to get the man by himself. But that would be hard to do because the man never went anywhere without the dogs.

One of the calves said she would change herself into a pretty young woman and make the man marry her. Then, she would tie the dogs so they couldn't go out, and then the man would be alone.

The next time the man went hunting in the woods, he was surprised to see a beautiful young woman. She was as pretty as red shoes with blue shoelaces. The man looked at her. She looked at him, and that took care of that.

Don't come asking me how a calf could turn itself into a woman. Back in them days animals could do all kinds of things they can't do now. At least, we don't think they can. But what do we know? I know some folks that act like animals and, for all I know, they might be.

Anyway, with the look the man gave her and the look she gave him, it wasn't long before they were looking at the preacher and saying, "I do."

They hadn't been married too long before the man announced that he would get up the next morning, take the dogs, and go hunting.

When he went to sleep, his wife took the dogs off in the woods and tied them to a big tree. The next morning the man couldn't find his dogs. He wasn't concerned because sometimes they went off by themselves. And if he needed them, all he had to do was call their names and no matter how far away they were, they would come running.

Off the man went into the woods.

The horned cattle saw him coming. When the man saw them, they ran. The man followed. Each time he came close, they ran and he followed. Deeper and deeper into the woods they went and deeper and deeper into the woods the man followed.

Finally the cattle came to a clearing. When the man arrived, it looked as if all the wild cattle in the world were there.

The man put an arrow in his bow and let it fly. At the same time he hollered for his dogs: "Minnyminny Morack! Follamalinska! Come, dogs! Come!"

He listened. He didn't hear the dogs coming. The man kept shooting at the cattle, but they moved out of the way of his arrows. Soon, the man was down to his last three arrows.

"Now we got you," the horned cattle said. "Let's see how you like it when we take *your* hide."

The man stuck one of his arrows in the ground. The arrow grew to be a huge tree, and the man was resting on the highest limb.

The horned cattle were angry now. They butted their heads against the tree. The tree didn't budge. They pawed and snorted. That might have made them feel better but it didn't do a thing to the tree. Some of the cattle got some axes and started cutting down the tree.

I understand you might not understand how cattle could cut a tree down with an axe. That's simple. If the cattle could talk and think, using an axe wasn't nothing. Now, if I'd said the cattle set the clock on my VCR, that would be unusual!

The man was sitting in the top of the tree, hollering, "Minnyminny Morack! Follamalinska! Come, dogs! Come!"

At the base of the tree, the horned cattle were chopping on the tree. "Blam! Blip-blip-blam! Blip-blip-blam!"

The tree started to shake. The man called the dogs, but they didn't come. The axes called the tree, and it came— right down to the ground—KERBLASHITY BLAM!

But the man stuck another arrow in the ground, and the tree grew up twice as tall and twice as big around as the first time.

"Minnyminny Morack! Follamalinska! Come, dogs! Come!"

The axes called the tree. "Down! Down! Dip-dip-down! Down-dip! Dip-down! Dippy-dip! Dippy-down!"

The dogs didn't come, but the tree did—KERBLASH-ITY BLAM!

The man stuck his last arrow in the ground and the tree grew up twice as tall and twice as big around as before.

The horned cattle started working their axes again. "Down! Down! Dip-dip-down! Down-dip! Dip-down! Dippy-dip! Dippy-down!"

"Minnyminny Morack! Follamalinska! Come, dogs! Come!"

The dogs could hear the man calling for them. They pulled at the ropes as hard as they could, but the ropes were big and strong. Finally, the dogs began chewing and gnawing on the ropes. Just as the last tree started to sway, the dogs got free.

The man heard them coming. "Minnyminny Morack! Follamalinska! Come, dogs! Come!"

The axes talked. "Tree-down! Tree-down! Trip-trip-tree-down!"

Just as the tree came down—KERBLASHITY BLAM!—the dogs rushed up. They did away with the horned cattle in a hurry.

When the dogs were finished, the man looked at the dead horned cattle and happened to notice a very pretty young cow.

When he went home, his wife wasn't there. He looked all over for her, but he never saw her again.

———————————————

"Cutta Cord-La"

One winter times got sho' 'nuf hard among the animals. The times was so hard that they didn't even get soft when spring sprung. And spring didn't sprang too high that year, 'cause they wasn't any rain. If there wasn't any rain, nothing grew. If nothing grew, there wasn't much for the animals to eat.

I don't know if you ever been hungry. I remember one time one of my children come running in the house and said, "I'm starved." I told him not to be using that word around me! No, sir! He don't know what starving is and never will.

Starving is when you don't have no food, and there is no food to be had. Starving is when you're too weak to cry, and if you could cry, there wouldn't be enough water inside you to make tears. But maybe the worst thing about starving is that it twists your mind. Just plain being hungry does funny things to my mind. You know what I mean? When I'm real hungry and you ask me a question, I might try to bite your head off. But when my belly is full, you ask me the same question, I'll be as nice as warm syrup on hot pancakes. Well, if being hungry makes you grouchy, starving can make you crazy. That's what happened to Brer Wolf.

One day he and Brer Rabbit were talking about how hungry they were and how they were afraid they might die.

"What we gon' do?" Brer Wolf asked.

Brer Rabbit sighed and shook his head. "Naw, we can't do that."

"Do what?"

Brer Rabbit shook his head again. "Forget I brought it up. It's just too gruesome to think about."

"How do I know it's gruesome if I can't think about it?"

Brer Rabbit sighed deeply. Then he started crying.

"What's the matter?" Brer Wolf wanted to know.

Brer Rabbit sniffed. "I don't know what else we can do except kill your grandmother."

Brer Wolf started crying.

The two of them cried for a while. Finally, Brer Wolf said, "I'm so hungry."

"Me too!" howled Brer Rabbit.

Brer Wolf got up, went home, and killed his grandmother. He took her body into town and sold it to a hunter. With the money he bought a lot of groceries and him and Brer Rabbit were able to eat for a while.

But the day came when the food ran out.

Brer Wolf said, "I ain't had nothing to eat in three days, Brer Rabbit. It's time for you to kill your grandmother."

Brer Rabbit looked at him like he was crazy. "It's time for me to do what? I can't kill my grandmother."

Brer Wolf was angry, very, very angry. "I'll make you kill your grandmother."

Brer Rabbit knew that Brer Wolf was serious. So, the first chance he got, Brer Rabbit sneaked away, took his grandmother, led her off in the woods, and hid her at the top of a coconut tree.

Don't come telling me that there're no coconut trees in the United States. There ain't none *now*! Back in them days, however, bananas grew in New York where the Empire State Building is now. That's what King Kong was looking for when he was up there with that skinny white woman.

Brer Rabbit gave his grandmother a basket with a cord tied to it and every morning he came to the tree and sang:

"Granny! Granny! O Granny! Jutta cord-la!"

When his grandmother heard his sweet voice, she would let the basket down with the cord, and Brer Rabbit would put in it whatever he had managed to find to eat. She would pull the cord and haul the basket up.

This was the routine, and every morning Brer Wolf watched from hiding. Finally, one day after Brer Rabbit left, Brer Wolf went to the base of the tree and sang out:

"Granny! Granny! O Granny! Shoot-a cord-la!"

Grandma Rabbit listened. "My grandson don't sound like that."

The next morning she told Brer Rabbit that somebody had come and sung, "Shoot-a cord-la." Brer Rabbit laughed because he knew who it had been.

When he left, Brer Wolf came out of hiding again.

"Granny! Granny! O Granny! Jutta cord-la!"

Grandma Rabbit listened. "You sound like you have a bad cold, Grandson. Your voice sound mighty rough." Grandma Rabbit peeped out of the tree and saw who it was. "Go 'way from here, Brer Wolf! You can't fool me! Go away!"

Brer Wolf was ten times mad now. He went off in the woods to think. Then he went to the blacksmith and asked him how he could get a fine voice like Brer Rabbit.

"Let me put this red hot poker down your throat. That'll make your voice smooth."

Brer Wolf gave his consent.

The blacksmith stuck the poker down Brer Wolf's throat. It hurt something fierce. When his throat was all healed, his voice was as smooth as chocolate pudding.

He went to the coconut tree.

"Granny! Granny! O Granny! Jutta cord-la!"

Grandmother Rabbit heard the voice and it sounded just like Brer Rabbit. She lowered the basket. Brer Wolf climbed in. Grandmother Rabbit started to pull.

"My! My! My grandson loves me so much that he bring me lots of food this time."

She pulled and just as the basket got close to the top, she stopped to rest.

Brer Wolf looked down. When he saw how far it was to the ground, his head started to swim. He looked up, and Grandmother Rabbit was staring at him with a strange smile on her face. He looked down again and there, at the base of the tree, was Brer Rabbit!

"Granny! Granny! O Granny! CUTTA CORD-LA!"

Brer Rabbit sang out.

Grandmother cut the cord. Brer Wolf dropped to the ground and broke his neck.

Brer Wolf was never hungry again.

Why Brer Bull Growls and Grumbles

I wonder what it was like back when animals could change themselves into people and back again. Goodness gracious! You wouldn't know whether you were talking to a person or buzzard. On the other hand, it must've been a lot of fun too. I probably would've turned myself into a cat so I could sleep all the time.

Brer Bull was lonely. All day he stood in the field and ate grass. How would you like to spend your life eating grass by yourself? Brer Bull was not only tired of being alone, he was also tired of eating grass. He decided to change himself into a man and find a wife.

There was a woman who lived with her son in a little

house on the other side of the road from the field where Brer Bull lived. Brer Bull changed himself into a man and showed up on the woman's doorstep, asking for a cool drink of water. Wasn't long after that but the man was at her house every night for supper.

The little boy's name was Simmy-Sam, and he was smart. He noticed that when the man came for supper, Brer Bull was not in the field. When Brer Bull was grazing in the field, the man was nowhere to be seen.

One day when Brer Bull was eating grass in the pasture, Simmy-Sam hid behind a tree and waited and watched. Close to suppertime, Brer Bull sat down like a dog. He shook his head and said, "Ballybaloobill!" His horns shrunk, his tail shriveled, and quicker than you can blink your eye, Brer Bull had become a man.

Simmy-Sam ran home so he could be there before the man came. All during supper, Simmy-Sam was quiet. He was afraid his mother was going to marry Brer Bull. His own daddy had died, but he didn't want a bull to be his new one.

A day or two later his momma told him she was going to marry the man.

"You can't do that, Momma," blurted Simmy-Sam. "You can't do that! He ain't no man. That's Brer Bull! I seen him change his shape. That's Brer Bull!"

His momma was in love, and when you in love, you wouldn't know sense if it walked up and hit you over the head with a brick.

His momma told him to stop making up stories or she would snatch him baldheaded. She left the hair on his head, but she didn't leave much skin on his bottom because she took a belt and gave Simmy-Sam a good whipping for telling tales.

Simmy-Sam didn't say anything. But every night when the man left the house, Simmy-Sam followed him. When the man got to the pasture, he said, "Billybalooball!" And the horns grew out of his head, and the hooves came out on his hands and feet. His clothes dropped off, and he was a bull again.

One evening when the man was sitting at the table eating supper, Simmy-Sam said, "Billybalooball!" The man put his hands up to his head, but there wasn't a thing he could do. The horns started to grow as his face changed into that of a bull; the hooves came out of his hands and feet; his clothes dropped off and before the man could get out

the door, he had changed into Brer Bull. His tail curled up on top of his back, and he ran to the pasture.

Simmy-Sam's mother apologized for thinking he was telling tales, but her apology didn't help his bottom much. Ain't no apology in the world ever made swelling go down or a bruise go away. Maybe it's better to be sorry *before* you hurt somebody.

Simmy-Sam was smart enough to know that Brer Bull was not done. Sure enough. Every time Simmy-Sam went to the yard to play, Brer Bull watched him.

Creatures are very patient. Brer Bull waited. He waited until the day Simmy-Sam's mother sent him into the woods to get kindling wood. She gave Simmy-Sam some pancakes to eat in case he got hungry.

Off Simmy-Sam went. Soon as he was deep in the woods, Brer Bull leaped over the fence and took off after him.

Simmy-Sam heard Brer Bull coming and climbed a tall tree. Brer Bull hit the tree with his horns—kerblip! He got a running start and hit the tree again—kerblam! Tree didn't move.

Guess what Brer Bull did then? Changed himself into a man. Guess what the man had in his hands? An axe!

"I got you now!" the man said, and he started in with the axe. "Come on down and save me the trouble of bringing you down."

"I'm scared."

"Scared or no scared, you better come down."

The man was chopping on the tree as fast as he could— blip! blap! blip! blap!

Simmy-Sam reached in the bag where the pancakes were. He dropped one on the man. The man's arm fell off. The man didn't stop to put the arm back on. He chopped with the arm he had left.

Simmy-Sam dropped another pancake on the man. His other arm fell off. The man couldn't cut anymore, but Simmy-Sam was still scared. So he dropped the last pancake, and the man's head fell off. Simmy-Sam climbed down and went home.

The man put all his body parts back on, changed himself back into a bull, and from that day to this, that is what he has remained. However, from that day to this, Brer Bull has growled and grumbled like somebody hurt his feelings.

And have you ever noticed that bulls don't like little children to come close to them? Well, now we know why.

Brer Rabbit, King Polecat, and the Gingercakes

Brer Polecat was king of all the creatures that run about after dark. You might have thought that Brer Lion was the king, and he was. But he was the king of all the creatures that run about in the morning, afternoon, evening, *and* night. Except that Brer Lion didn't like to be awakened at night to do any kinging, and that's when Brer Polecat took over.

Brer Rabbit noticed how much Brer Polecat enjoyed kinging. It seemed to him that Brer Polecat might enjoy it a little *too* much.

One afternoon when King Polecat and all the animals were together, Brer Rabbit cleared his throat. "Hear! Hear! I have an announcement to make!"

Everybody gathered around to listen. "I think every creature, winged and paw, feathered and skin, can agree that when it comes to kinging, can't nobody do it better than Brer Polecat."

The creatures certainly agreed with that.

"Seeing as how that is the case, I propose a new law. Every time any of us meet Brer Polecat in the road we have to shut our eyes and hold our nose."

The creatures thought that was a good idea except some of them weren't too eager to shut their eyes.

"If I close my eyes, Brer Hawk might eat me," said Brer Mouse.

"If I close my eyes, I might walk into a a tree," Brer Bear put in.

"If I close my eyes, I might go to sleep," said Brer Dog.

Brer Rabbit ignored their objections. "Seems to me there ain't no risk too big to honor such a king as Brer Polecat."

So, it was agreed. Anytime any of the creatures saw Brer Polecat in the road, they would close their eyes and hold their noses until he had passed.

Brer Polecat lived in a big house with Brer Coon and Brer Mink. Brer Coon was known far and wide for the gingercakes he made. There wasn't a party or function of any kind held without a stack of Brer Coon's gingercakes being served.

If Brer Rabbit thought about Brer Coon, his stomach started growling for gingercakes. That's what happened the very next morning after the new law was passed. Brer Rabbit thought about Brer Coon and his stomach started growling. Brer Rabbit headed for Brer Coon's.

When he got there, he bought a stack of gingercakes. He was getting ready to eat them when he remembered that he didn't have any garlic to eat them with. Brer Coon said he didn't like garlic on his, so he didn't have any.

"Please watch my gingercakes," Brer Rabbit asked Brer Coon. "I'm going to hurry home and get some garlic."

Brer Coon said he would and off Brer Rabbit went.

Brer Rabbit was hardly out of sight before King Polecat showed up. Brer Coon shut his eyes and held his nose. Brer Polecat ate the gingercakes Brer Rabbit had just bought, and off he went.

A little later, Brer Rabbit came lippitin' back with the garlic. "Brer Coon? You said you would watch my gingercakes."

Brer Coon didn't know what to say. "I didn't see anybody take them."

Brer Rabbit wasn't too happy, but his stomach wanted some gingercakes real bad. He ran his hand in his pocket and bought another stack.

"I got my garlic with me, so I'll watch these gingercakes my own self."

Brer Rabbit sat down, pulled out his knife and fork, and put some garlic on the cakes. Just as he was about to do away with that stack, here come King Polecat.

Brer Rabbit jumped up, held his nose and shut his eyes. Well, not really. A rabbit's eyes are so big that he can't shut them all the way. So as soon as King Polecat reached for the gingercakes, Brer Rabbit hollored, "Drop them cakes!"

King Polecat jumped back. "You didn't play fair, Brer Rabbit! Your eyes were supposed to be shut! No fair! No fair!"

Brer Rabbit apologized and explained that he couldn't shut his eyes. "Give me back my gingercakes or I'll tell all the creatures what a low-down thief you are and then you won't be king anymore."

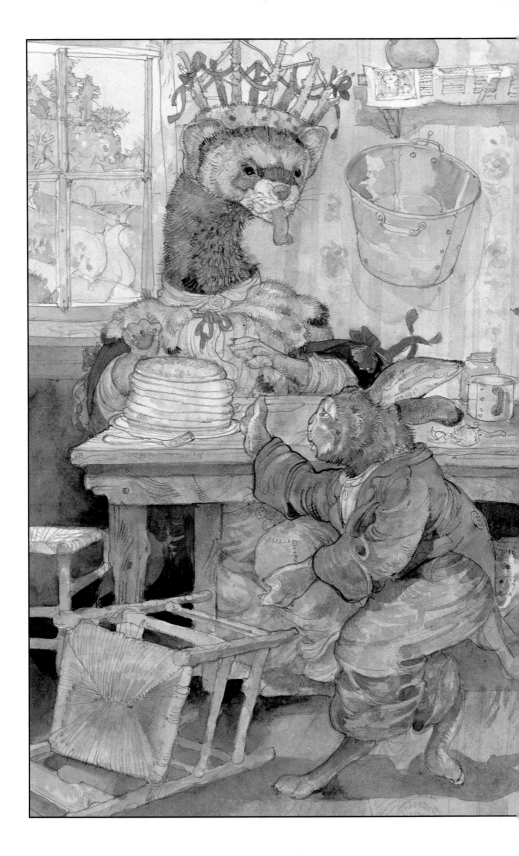

King Polecat was angry, but what could he do? If he was going to be king, he had to stay on Brer Rabbit's good side. Of course, when all the creatures saw how nice Brer Polecat treated Brer Rabbit, always asking his advice, they understood who was *really* king.

The Fool

Once there was a man who acted strange. Some mornings he put on one shoe and forgot the other and walked around all day with one shoe on and the other foot bare and he never noticed. Folks said he was cripple under his hat. But he worked hard, and when he finished his harvesting he had a crib full of corn. Every morning when he went out to admire his corn, the pile seemed to be a little lower than it had been the day before.

The fool watched his corn day and night and didn't see even an ear disappear, but the pile kept getting lower and lower.

The fool lived on the river. On the other side of the river was a deep woods. Somebody told the fool that squirrels were crossing the river, taking his corn, and hiding it in the woods.

The fool laughed. "If the squirrels can carry off my corn, they're welcome to it."

The fool got up early the next morning to see what he could see. Wasn't long before the squirrels came. They climbed in the crib, took an ear of corn, and started for the river.

When they got there, they took pieces of bark, put the corn on the bark, and perched on top of the corn. They raised their tails like sails and went across the river.

The fool could not believe his eyes. The next morning he watched. The same thing happened. Each squirrel took an ear of corn, laid it on a piece of bark, climbed on top, raised his tail and sailed on across.

The fool thought that squirrels were the most clever creatures he had ever seen. He laughed and laughed and told his neighbors what the squirrels were doing.

They asked him why he didn't stop them from stealing his corn.

He winked and grinned.

"You the biggest fool around here," they told him.

He winked and laughed.

With the squirrels coming every morning and taking his corn, it wasn't long before the fool didn't have much corn left. So, one morning he took his gun and his axe and went across the river to get his corn back.

He hadn't been looking for the squirrels long, before a rabbit jumped out of the woods. The fool raised his gun and fired. The rabbit ran into a covey of partridges. The sound of the gun scared a turkey, who flew up in a big tree. The man fired the other barrel, and the turkey fell dead across a tree limb.

The fool looked around and saw one dead rabbit, eleven dead partridges, and up in the tree a dead turkey. One partridge wasn't dead, though, and it ran off into the bushes. The fool followed, and what should he come upon but a nest of turkey eggs.

He took the turkey eggs and then climbed the tree to get the dead turkey. When he climbed up there, however, the turkey had dropped into a hole in the tree. The fool pulled the turkey out and guess what was in the hole? His corn!

The fool climbed down, took his axe, and started to chop down the tree. He hadn't been chopping long, before he noticed something sticky oozing out of the tree. He tasted it. You know what it was? Wasn't nothing but honey!

The fool plugged up the hole to keep the honey from oozing out. He picked up the dead rabbit, dead turkey, eleven dead partridges, and the turkey eggs, and started for home. As he was walking through the woods, another rabbit jumped out in front of him. The fool's gun wasn't loaded, so he threw it at the rabbit but missed.

The man went to pick up his gun, and the ground beneath his feet gave away. The next thing he knew he was in a dark hole. He felt around and touched something hard and cold. You know what it was? That's right! A barrel of money!

The hole wasn't that deep so the man lifted the barrel of money out and rolled it down to the river and loaded it on his canoe. When he got home he counted the money and discovered he was a rich man! There was forty-'leven thousand dollars in that barrel.

The next day the fool hitched up his horse and wagon and drove the long way around and went over the bridge to cross the river. He had some empty barrels in the wagon, and he filled them with the honey. The day after that he came back with more barrels and filled them with all the corn that was in the tree. There was a lot of corn in that tree because the squirrels had been stealing from more folks than him.

Just think. If the man hadn't been a fool, he never would've gotten rich.

How Brer Lion Lost His Hair

The lion might be the king of all the animals, but, if you ask me, I've always thought the lion was kind of funny looking. He has a lot of hair around his head and a little on his tail. But in between head and tail, why, he's buck naked.

That wasn't how the Lord made him. Uh-uh. Brer Lion used to be hairy all over. He had so much hair it drug on the ground like a cape. That's how come the Lion was king. Anybody with that much pretty hair couldn't be expected to do no work. Well, here's how the lion lost his hair.

One day over in the autumn, right after the first frost, Mr. Man knew it was hog-killing time. He laid wood in a pile and put rocks between the wood. Then he lay the barrel across the wood and the rocks at an angle, and set the wood on fire. He killed the hogs and took the rocks he had set between the wood. They were red-hot now, and he threw them in the barrel of water. Before long the water started boiling. Mr. Man soused the hogs in the water. When he took them out, the hair on the hogs was ready to drop off. Mr. Man scraped the hides until no hair was left.

After Mr. Man had soused and scraped all the hogs and took them to the barn where he would cure the meat, and everything was as still as a setting hen, Brer Rabbit came out from behind a bush. He went over to the fire to warm his hands.

He hadn't been there long before Brer Wolf and Brer Fox came along.

"Hello, friends," Brer Rabbit greeted them. "Howdy and welcome! I was just getting ready to take a warm bath like Mr. Man just gave his hogs. Would you care to join me?"

Brer Wolf and Brer Fox treated water like they treated work—they wouldn't go near it.

"Well, would you help me put these hot rocks in the barrel?"

They didn't see any harm in doing that. Soon, the water in the barrel was bubbling again. About that time, here come Brer Lion.

He growled. "What y'all doing?"

"I was just getting ready to take a bath," Brer Rabbit answered.

"That's what I need," Brer Lion roared. "How do I do it?"

"Just back right in," Brer Rabbit told him.

Brer Lion backed in. The water was hot, very, very hot. Brer Lion roared the loudest roar a lion would ever roar. AAAAAAAAARRRRRRRRRRRRRRGGGGGGGG-GGGGHHHHHHHHHHHHHHHH!!!!!!!!!!!! He scrambled trying to get out of that barrel, but he slipped in deeper, until he was in up to his shoulder blades.

When he finally got out, all the hair dropped off his body, except that around his neck and head and a little bit at the end of his tail. The only reason he had any hair there was because the end of his tail had been sticking out of a hole in the barrel.

He was a funny sight, but because he was the king, the animals didn't laugh at him. At least, not while he was in hearing range.

The Man and the Boots

There was a man who had a pair of new boots with red tops. He was sitting beside the road when he heard a wagon coming. He hid in a ditch and watched the wagon go by. It was filled with all kinds of things—new dishes, a VCR, a microwave, and a popcorn popper. The man with the boots wanted all them things for himself.

He ran through the woods until he was ahead of the

wagon. He took one of his boots and threw it in the road. Then he hid in the bushes to see what the man in the wagon would do.

In a few minutes the man in the wagon came along, saw the boot, and told his mule, "Whoa!" He looked at the boot and thought for a minute.

"If there were two of you, I'd take you. But one boot can't do me no good, not if I ain't got one wooden leg. Giddap!" And he drove on.

The man who owned the boots ran through the woods until he was ahead of the man in the wagon again. He threw the other boot in the road.

When the man in the wagon came along and saw this boot, he said, "Whoa! It looks like I'm in business. This boot makes the first one good for a man with two legs of flesh and bone." He jumped off the wagon and went back down the road to find the other boot.

As soon as he did, the man who owned the boots came out from hiding and took the VCR and the popcorn popper and the other things and hid in the woods with them.

Before long the man who owned the wagon came back. He had two boots now, but that was all he had. His wagon was empty! He didn't say anything. He didn't even act shocked or surprised.

He climbed in the wagon and started laughing. He looked in the boots and laughed harder.

The man who had put the boots in the road couldn't understand what was so funny about the boots.

He sneaked through the woods and came walking down the road toward the man in the wagon. The man in the wagon was laughing so hard, tears were coming down his face.

"I ain't never seen a man have so much fun by himself," the thief said to the man in the wagon.

"Well, if you had these boots, you would be happy too!"

The man in the road furrowed his brow. "What's wrong with the boots?"

"Not a thing! Not a thing!" the man in the wagon said, and started laughing again.

"You ain't losing your mind, are you?"

The man in the wagon said, "Well, if you were driving along a road and found what I found in them boots, you would be laughing just as hard."

The man in the road said, "I had a pair of boots just like them, and they didn't make me laugh."

"I guess the boots you had didn't have thousand-dollar bills inside them."

"Let me see them boots! Let me see them boots! I bet they're mine. You hand them over right now. I lost them boots yesterday."

"Are you sure these are your boots?" the man in the wagon asked.

"Absolutely, positively, and certainly. I got proof!"

The man in the wagon said, "Well, come up here and show me your proof."

The man in the road climbed up in the wagon but before he could do or say anything, the man in the wagon flung him down, tied him up, and carried him to town, where he handed him over to the high sheriff. There the man confessed to taking the VCR and the popcorn popper and the other stuff, and he had to make his home in jail for a long time after that.

Of course, the man in the wagon hadn't found anything in them boots. What the man who owned the boots didn't understand was that it's all right when the creatures take what don't belong to them, and play loose with the truth. They are creatures. But when folks try it, they will come to a bad end every time.

Why the Goat Has a Short Tail

Brer Billy Goat and Brer Dog were promenading around and being sociable one day when, suddenly, a big rainstorm came up.

"I left my umbrella at home," Brer Billy Goat said.

"Rain don't bother me," Brer Dog said.

"Well, I don't like the rain," Brer Billy Goat said and trotted as fast as he could until he came to a house. Brer Dog went along with him.

Brer Billy Goat knocked on the door and said, "Baaaaaa!"

Brer Dog wagged his tail and said, "Arf! Arf! Arf!"

The peephole in the door opened, and guess whose house it was? Brer Wolf! He looked at Brer Billy Goat and Brer Dog out there in the rain. "Well, well, well. Why don't you all come in out of the wet?"

Brer Dog shook his head and began kicking up dirt and gravel with his back two legs. You know why? He smelled blood from inside Brer Wolf's house. Brer Billy Goat saw how Brer Dog was acting and he decided that he shouldn't go in either.

"Come in and sit by the fire and dry yourselves off," Brer Wolf implored.

Brer Billy Goat and Brer Dog shook their heads.

Brer Wolf thought that if he could get Brer Billy Goat and Brer Dog to dancing, then he could get them in the house and have them for dinner. He took down his fiddle and started in to playing. Brer Billy Goat wouldn't dance.

Finally, Brer Wolf asked, "Tell me something. How do you all get meat?"

"I depend on my teeth," Brer Billy Goat said.

"Me too," answered Brer Dog.

"Well, I depend on my four feet," Brer Wolf said, and he opened the door and started after Brer Billy Goat and Brer Dog.

Off they went through the rain. They ran until they came to a big creek.

"What we going to do?" Brer Billy Goat asked Brer Dog.

"I'm going to swim," Brer Dog responded.

Brer Billy Goat started to cry. "I can't swim a lick."

Brer Dog said, "Don't worry." He reached in his pocket and pulled out a rabbit's foot. He touched Brer Billy Goat with it. Brer Billy Goat turned into a white rock. Brer Dog leaped into the creek and swam across.

Brer Wolf came up about that time, but he was scared of the water. Brer Dog was on the other bank now and he hollered over, "You look like you scared, Brer Wolf. You made Brer Billy Goat drown, but you scared of me. I dare you to throw that white rock at me!"

Brer Wolf was mad. He reached down, picked up the rock and threw it as hard as he could at Brer Dog. The instant the rock hit the ground it turned into Brer Billy Goat.

Brer Billy Goat shook himself a time or two and then hollered, "What you trying to do? Break my neck?"

Then, Brer Billy Goat looked at himself, and that's when

he noticed that his long tail had broken off when he hit the ground. But he was so happy that the rest of him was all right that he didn't mind one bit. Not one bit.

Brer Buzzard and Brer Crow

One day Brer Buzzard and Brer Crow found themselves perched in the same tree together. They spoke politely, but that was about it.

Brer Crow had heard that Brer Buzzard had been going through the community bragging about how he could outfly Brer Crow. Before long Brer Buzzard said that very thing to Brer Crow's face.

"Can't do much flying with them squinchy wings of yours, can you?"

A crow ain't no sparrow-sized bird, if you know what I mean. Their wings make a nice-sized shadow. But compared to Brer Buzzard's, they were not large at all.

They got to arguing back and forth and forth and back about whose wings could stir up the most wind and who could fly the farthest and who could fly the fastest and who could fly the highest, and someone would've called the police if there had been any to call.

Finally, Brer Crow admitted, "You can probably outfly me, Brer Buzzard, but I know this. You can't outsing me."

"How you know? I ain't never tried."

"I'll bet you a new suit and a hat that I can sit here and sing longer than you can."

"Let's get to it," Brer Buzzard declared.

"Not so fast. I just thought of something. This ain't a fair bet because you are bigger than I am. You got a bigger wind chamber and can hold more air, and therefore, you can probably sing longer than me. Well, no matter. I'm going to beat you singing if I die trying."

They shook hands and Brer Crow shut his eyes and started singing:

> *Susu! susu! gangook!*
> *Mother, mother, lalho!*

Brer Buzzard shut his eyes and he started in to singing:

> *Susu! susu! gangook!*
> *Mother, mother, lalho!*

Don't come asking me what the song was about. That's the way it was given to me. If you can get on the inside of it, more power to you. If you can't, don't fling none of

the blame on me. Young as you are, you know just as much about that song as I do and probably more, because you ain't been trying to figure it out as long as I have.

They sang and they sang. Brẹr Buzzard would stop for a minute every now and then to catch his breath and then he would go right back to it:

Susu! susu! gangook!
Mother, mother, lalho!

Brer Crow would stop to catch his breath and then he would go back to it:

Susu! susu! gangook!
Mother, mother, lalho!

It went on like this until they both began to get hungry. But Brer Buzzard was the biggest, and it looked like he was going to win the contest. Brer Crow was very hungry, and his voice was getting weak, but he hadn't given up.

Somewhere between hungriness and starvation Brer Crow saw Miss Crow flying over. He sang out as loud as he could, "*Susu!* go tell my children—*susu!*—to bring my dinner—*gangook!*—and tell them—*mother, mother*—to bring it quick—*lalho!*"

Wasn't long before the Crow family brought Brer Crow more food than he could eat. Brer Crow got his strength back and he sang so loud his kin began to wish they had let him starve.

As for Brer Buzzard, well, he didn't have no kin to bring him any food, but he wasn't about to lose the contest. He sang and he sang. He got hungrier and hungrier. He got weaker and weaker. Finally he dropped out of the tree.

You know? There're folks who would rather die than lose.

The Blacksmith and the Devil

I was sitting here thinking about the days when the creatures and the people could talk to one another, the days when creatures could turn into people and back again. Don't none of that go on anymore, and you know why? There ain't no more darkness.

Think about it! In the cities where most people live, night don't never come. Things go from daytime to neon time. And it never gets quiet. You can't hear a cricket sing if it's noisy. And you can't see a Jacky-My-Lantern in neon time.

I saw a Jacky-My-Lantern once when I was growing up down South. I was coming along the big road on my way home. Where I had been and what I was doing is my business! Suddenly I saw this strange light hovering off at the edge of the woods. It looked like lightning bugs, but the light burned more intensely. It looked like it wanted me to follow it. I knew better than that. You follow a Jacky-My-Lantern, you won't come to the dinner table anymore. This is the story my daddy told me about where the Jacky-My-Lantern come from.

One time there was a blacksmith. This blacksmith was an evil man. He was so evil that red roses turned green when he walked by. He was so evil that rain turned to steam when it tried to fall on him. He was so evil that his shadow walked a block behind, so as not to be seen with him.

Word about the blacksmith got down to the Devil. Sounded like the kind of man whose acquaintance he wouldn't mind making. The Devil said the magic formula that only he knew, and his horns and tail and hooves disappeared and he dressed up in a suit and tie and appeared at the blacksmith's door.

"I don't care who you are or what you want!" the blacksmith said to his visitor. "Get out of my face!"

The Devil liked that. "I heard you were almost as evil as me."

"I'm so evil the grass asks my permission before it grows. And if I tell it no, it won't come up."

The Devil laughed. "You are definitely my kind of man."

The blacksmith was curious. "And who might you be?"

"I'm the Devil, and I've come to take you back to hell with me. I can use your talents."

The blacksmith preferred to use his talents on earth. He begged and pleaded and cried. "Please, Mr. Devil. Please don't take me! Let me stay right on earth where I can do your work for you. I'm more beneficial to you here."

The Devil thought it over. That was true. "I'll make you a proposition. You can live for one more year if you do as much evil as any man has ever done."

"You just watch me!"

The Devil was pleased. "To help you in your work, I'm going to give you something." The Devil put a spell on the blacksmith's chair and his sledgehammer. "Anybody who sits in your chair will be stuck there until you tell the chair to let him go. Any man who picks up your sledge-hammer will have to pound with the hammer until you tell the hammer to quit." Then he gave the blacksmith enough money to last him a year even if he spent a hundred dollars a day. Then the Devil disappeared.

The blacksmith had a year that was not soon forgotten. If folks enjoyed doing good as much as the blacksmith enjoyed doing evil, the world would be free of problems.

The blacksmith was having so much fun doing evil that he forgot about the contract he had made with the Devil. He forgot until he looked out the window one morning. There was the Devil coming up the road. The blacksmith looked at the calendar and the year was up that day.

The Devil came in the house without knocking on the door. To tell the truth, the Devil came in without even *opening* the door. The blacksmith was pounding on a horseshoe and didn't pay the Devil no mind.

"It's time to go," the Devil announced.

"Give me a couple of minutes to finish up these jobs here."

"Ain't got time."

"What's the hurry? Ten minutes ain't gon' make that much difference, is it?"

"Compared to eternity, I guess not."

"There you go. Sit down in that chair and take it easy. I won't be long."

The Devil sat down in the chair, the same chair he had put the spell on. There he was, stuck. Blacksmith laughed and laughed. Devil tried to get up, but the chair held him tight.

Finally, the blacksmith made the Devil a proposition. "Tell you what. I'll let you out of the chair if you'll give me another year."

What could the Devil do? So the deal was struck. The Devil went back to hell, and the blacksmith had another year to do evil.

The year went by so fast that the morning the blacksmith looked out the window and saw the Devil coming up the road he was sure somebody had stolen some pages off his calendar. But when he checked, they were all there. Time goes by so fast when you're having a good time, don't it?

"Let's go!" the Devil said. "And no, I am not going to sit down and wait until you finish what you're doing. The year's up, and you're coming with me this minute."

The blacksmith was beating on a piece of iron with his sledgehammer. "Well, all right," he said, resigned to his fate. He handed the Devil the sledge.

Without thinking the Devil took it, and remembered too late that he had cursed the hammer.

The hammer started hammering. It flung the Devil this way and that, that way and this, up and down, side to side, round and round. The blacksmith laughed and laughed.

"Give me one more year, and I'll tell the hammer to stop!"

"You got it!" the Devil hollered.

That year passed by quickly. The morning the Devil came for the blacksmith, there wasn't a thing the blacksmith could do. The Devil grabbed him and stuffed him in a sack and off down the road he went.

He hadn't gone far before he passed a lot of people at a barbecue. The Devil knew there had to be at least one evil person at a barbecue, so he stopped to see if he could find him. He put the sack underneath a table and began to mingle with the people.

As soon as the sack hit the ground, the blacksmith began to work his way out. Soon he was free. He saw a large bulldog. He stuffed it in the sack and sneaked away.

The Devil came back for his sack. He had found a lot of evil folks at the barbecue, but they needed ripening. He'd come back in a year or two.

He slung the sack over his shoulder and headed for hell. When he got there, his children came running up to him. "Who'd you bring back today, Daddy?"

"The most evil man on earth."

"Ooooo! Let's see him!"

The Devil untied the sack and the bulldog charged out, grabbed the Devil's children, and had almost done away with them before the Devil got a hold on him and dragged him outside the gates.

The years went by. The blacksmith was on the topside of the world doing evil. Finally, he choked to death on his bad breath.

The blacksmith didn't mind being dead because now he had eternal life. He just wasn't sure where he was supposed to live it. He went up to Heaven and rang the doorbell on the Pearly Gate. Saint Peter looked through the peephole, saw who it was, and said, "Get away from here! Get away!"

The blacksmith headed to hell. He rang the doorbell on the gate down there. The Devil looked through his peephole, saw who it was, and said, "I know you! I know you! If I let you in here, next thing I know I'll be working for you. Get away from here! Get away!"

Since that time the blacksmith has been wandering between Heaven and earth, looking for a home. Folks out in the country say on dark nights you can see him hovering at the edge of woods and swamps looking for somebody to go home with. But he hasn't found anybody yet.

Why Chickens Scratch in the Dirt

There were two large farms next to each other. One time the chickens and fowls on one place decided to throw a big party and invite the chickens and fowls from the other farm.

They sent invitations, and the other chickens and fowls sent back their RSVPs saying that not only were they coming, but they were bringing their appetites.

The day of the party came. The chickens and fowls who were the *invitees* were all excited. Mr. Rooster blew his horn and assembled them together and off they marched, Mr. Rooster in the lead, his head held high. Behind him was Miss Hen and behind her was Miss Pullet, and next was Mr. Peafowl and Mr. Turkey Gobbler and Miss Guinea Hen and Miss Puddle Duck, and then all their aunts and cousins and children and whomsoever else was in the fowl family. They marched out of their barnyard, across the field, down alongside the creek, up the hill, past the corral and the outhouse, and before long, they were there.

The fowls what done the inviting were happy to see

everybody, and they proceeded to have themselves a party. They danced and sang for a long time. Their favorite song was the one that went like this:

Come under, come under,
My honey, my love, my own true love,
My heart been a-weeping
Way down in Galilee.

They partied and sang and danced until they were hot and thirsty. Mr. Peafowl blew on the dinner horn, and everybody went and washed their faces and hands and went in for dinner.

All they saw was a big table. On it there was nothing but a pile of corn bread. Mr. Rooster looked at the corn bread and put his head in the air. He was insulted that there wasn't anything more, and he strutted out.

All the fowl who had come with him were upset. Miss Hen and Miss Pullet cackled and squalled; Mr. Gobbler, well, he gobbled. Miss Puddle Duck shook her tail and said, "*Quickty-quack-quack.*"

Mr. Rooster wouldn't change his mind, though.

The other fowl didn't know what to do. Should they walk out with Mr. Rooster? Before they could seriously consider the matter, however, their gullets had a thing or two to say, and what their gullets said was, "Let's eat!" And that's what they did.

They started pecking at the corn bread and before too many pecks they made a discovery. Underneath the corn bread was a whole pile of hot meat and greens and baked sweet potatoes and okra.

Mr. Rooster was outside and heard all these noises coming from inside. He peeked through a crack. When he saw

how much food was under that corn bread, he felt mighty foolish. Some of the other fowls went out to him and begged him to come in and get some of the food. But he was too proud.

He learned his lesson, though. From that day to this, chickens peck and scratch before, during, and after they eat, just to be sure that what they see is all there is.

Brer Rabbit and Aunt Nancy

Once a year all the creatures—winged and claw, big and little, long-tail, bobtail, and no-tail—had to go see Aunt Nancy. Aunt Nancy was the great-grandmother of the Witch-Rabbit, Mammy-Bammy-Big-Money. She ruled all the animals, even King Lion. When she wanted them to know that she was watching their every move, all she had to do was suck in her breath and the creatures would get a chill.

One year it came time for the creatures to go pay their respects.

"I ain't going!" Brer Rabbit announced.

"You got to go," the other animals argued with him.

"Says who? I don't feel like going way up in the country and into that thick swamp just to see Aunt Nancy."

"You better go," they told him.

"I done already been and seen. But, when you get where you going, ask Aunt Nancy to shake hands with you. Then you'll see what I saw."

The creatures went off. After a while they came to Aunt Nancy's house. If you had seen her house, you would've said it looked like a big chunk of fog.

Brer Bear hollered, "Hallooooo!"

Aunt Nancy came out wearing a big black cloak and sat down on a pine stump. Her eyeballs sparkled red like they were on fire.

"Let me call the roll to be sure everybody is here," she said in a voice like chalk on a blackboard.

"Brer Wolf!"

"Here!"

"Brer Possum!"

"Here!"

Finally she got to the last one. "Brer Rabbit!"

Silence.

"Brer Rabbit!"

More silence.

"BRER RABBIT!!!!!"

Silence and more silence.

"Did Brer Rabbit send an excuse as to why he ain't here?" Aunt Nancy asked the creatures.

Brer Wolf said, "No, he didn't."

Brer Bear added, "He said to tell you howdy and he told us to tell you to shake hands with us and remember him in your dreams."

Aunt Nancy rolled her eyes and chomped her lips together. "Is that what he told you? Well, you tell him that if he'll come, I'll shake hands with him. Tell him that if he don't come, then I'll come and shake hands with him where he lives."

Brer Bear persisted. "Why won't you shake hands with us? You're hurting my feelings."

Aunt Nancy rolled her eyes again. She got up. But her cloak got caught on the tree stump and slipped off. The creatures looked. She was half woman and half spider, with seven arms and no hands. That's why her house looked like fog. It was a web.

The creatures got away from there as fast as their legs could take them.

When they got back and told Brer Rabbit what they had seen, he chuckled but didn't say a word.

That was the last time the animals went to see Aunt Nancy.

The Adventures of Simon and Susanna

Once upon a time there was a man who had a very beautiful daughter named Susanna. Susanna was so beautiful that all the young men wanted to marry her.

Her father sent out the word that the man who could clear six acres of land, cut all the wood into logs, and pile up all the underbrush in one day could marry his daughter.

Nobody could do something like that, and even if he could, the question was if he would. And if he could've and would've, Susanna wasn't worth that much work.

There was one young man, however, who thought she was. His name was Simon. Simon loved Susanna. Susanna loved Simon. That made it convenient for both of them.

Simon went to Susanna's father. "I accept your challenge. If any man can clear that land, cut the trees into logs, and pile up the brush in one day, I am the man."

The father grinned. "We'll see about that tomorrow."

What Simon did not know was that the man was a witch. But what the man did not know was that his daughter had learned all of his tricks and had a few of her own.

The next morning when Simon came by the house, Susanna got an axe for him. She sprinkled black sand on it and said, "Axe, cut. Cut, axe." Then she rubbed her hair across the axe, gave it to Simon, and said, "Go down to the creek and get seven white pebbles, put them in this little cloth bag I'm giving you, and whenever you want the axe to cut, shake the pebbles in the bag."

Simon got the seven white pebbles and put them in the cloth bag Susanna had given him. Then he went off in the woods and shook the bag. The axe started cutting. As the trees fell they broke up into logs and rolled themselves into piles, while the brush uprooted itself and fell into piles.

About two hours before sundown, the man came down to see how Simon was doing. He almost fainted when he saw the six acres cleared, the logs and brush piled up, and

Simon sitting down, his back resting against a stack of logs.

The man didn't know what to say. He didn't want to give up Susanna, but he didn't know how to get out of it. He walked around and around, thinking and thinking.

"You're a mighty good worker," he said finally.

"Yessir! When I start a job, I don't stop until I get it done."

"Well, since you got so much energy, there's two more acres across the creek. Get them cleared up before supper and you can come to the house and get Susanna."

"I'll get right to it."

Simon took the axe and the bag of pebbles across the

creek. He shook the bag, and the axe set to work. The two acres were cleared and all the wood and brush piled up, and there was still an hour to go before supper.

Simon went to the house and knocked on the front door. "I'm finished."

The man went down to see for himself. Sure enough, the two acres were clear. He came back to the house and called Susanna. "Looks like you gon' have to marry Simon tomorrow."

But the man still didn't want to let his daughter go. That night he told her that after she and Simon got married they had to go upstairs to the front room and she had to make Simon get in the bed first.

The man went upstairs and sawed the floor under the bed in the front room until the floor was weak. When Simon got in the bed, the floor would give away. The bed and Simon would go through, and Simon would be killed.

The next evening Simon and Susanna were married, and they went upstairs and into the front room. As soon as they were inside Susanna grabbed Simon's hand and put one finger to her lips to tell him to talk softly.

"We got to run away from here before daddy kills both of us," she whispered. "Pick up your hat and button up your coat. Now, take this stick of wood from behind the door and hold it above your head."

Susanna got a hen egg, a meal-bag, and a skillet. "Drop the wood on the bed."

Simon did so. The bed went crashing through the floor. Susanna grabbed Simon's hand and they ran down the back stairs and out the back door.

Her father heard the bed come crashing through the ceiling. He ran into the room, expecting to see Simon lying there, dead. But there was no Simon. He ran upstairs. There was no Simon *or* Susanna.

He was mad now. He ran outside and saw Simon and Susanna running down the road, holding each other's hands. He grabbed his knife and took out after them.

Before long he was close enough to smell their fear. And that's when Susanna said to Simon, "Drop your coat!"

Simon flung his coat to the ground. A thick woods sprang up. Her father cut his way through it with his knife and had soon caught up to Simon and Susanna again.

Susanna dropped the egg on the ground. A big fog rose up, and her father was lost for a while. He conjured up a wind to blow the fog away and was soon after Simon and Susanna again.

As he got close, Susanna dropped the meal-sack and a large pond of water covered the ground where it fell. The man drank as much of the pond as he could. Then he blew his hot breath on it and dried it up and took out after Simon and Susanna again.

They were running as fast and as hard as they could. But no matter how fast or how hard they ran, her father ran faster and harder. As he got close again, Susanna dropped the skillet. A big bank of darkness fell, and the man didn't know which way to go. He conjured up light to suck the darkness up and took after Simon and Susanna again.

"Drop a pebble," Susanna told Simon.

He did so, and a hill rose up, but her father climbed the hill and kept gaining on them.

"Drop another pebble."

Simon dropped another one, and a mountain grew up. Her father climbed it and kept gaining on them.

"Drop the biggest pebble!"

A big rock wall rose up. It was so high, her father got a crick in his neck trying to see the top of it. He ran along the wall but he couldn't see to the end of it. He ran along the wall in the other direction but couldn't see to the end that way either. He couldn't go over and he couldn't go around. There wasn't a thing for him to do but to go home.

Simon and Susanna went their way and from what I heard, they lived happily ever after.

And I hope you do too.

ABOUT THE AUTHOR

Julius Lester is the author of books for both young people and adults. His first three retellings of Uncle Remus stories, *The Tales of Uncle Remus, More Tales of Uncle Remus,* and *Further Tales of Uncle Remus,* have received many awards and honors, including three ALA Notables; two Coretta Scott King Honors; as well as two *Booklist* Editors' Choices; *American Bookseller* Picks of the Lists, *School Library Journal* Best Books, two Parents' Choice Awards; and three NCSS Notable Children's Books in the Field of Social Sciences. Mr. Lester's other books for Dial include the ground-breaking *To Be a Slave,* a Newbery Honor Book and ALA Notable; *Long Journey Home: Stories from Black History,* a National Book Award finalist; *This Strange New Feeling,* an NCSS Notable Book in the Field of Social Studies; and *The Knee-High Man and Other Tales,* an ALA Notable Book, *School Library Journal* Best Book of the Year, and Lewis Carroll Shelf Award winner. His adult books include *Do Lord Remember Me,* a *New York Times* Notable Book, and *Lovesong: Becoming a Jew,* a National Jewish Book Award finalist.

Mr. Lester was born in St. Louis and grew up in Kansas City, Kansas, and Nashville, Tennessee, where he received his Bachelor of Arts from Fisk University. He is the father of four children. He lives in western Massachusetts and teaches at the University of Massachusetts at Amherst.

Jerry Pinkney, a two-time Caldecott Honor Book artist, is the only illustrator ever to have won the Coretta Scott King Award for Illustration three times. *Back Home,* written by Gloria Jean Pinkney, his wife, was a 1992 ALA Notable Book and *Booklist* Editors' Choice. *The Talking Eggs,* by Robert D. San Souci, was a Caldecott Honor Book and won the Coretta Scott King Award. Valerie Flournoy's *The Patchwork Quilt* received numerous awards, including the Coretta Scott King Award, the Christopher Award, and it was also an IRA–CBC Children's Choice, an ALA Notable Book, and a *Reading Rainbow* Feature Selection. Mr. Pinkney's other books for Dial include *I Want to Be* by Thylias Moss, *The Sunday Outing* by Gloria Jean Pinkney, and *David's Songs: His Psalms and Their Story* selected and edited by Colin Eisler.

Mr. Pinkney has taught art at the University of Delaware. He is the recent recipient of the Hamilton King Award of the Society of Illustrators in New York, the David McCord Award from Framingham State College, and the Drexel Citation for Children's Literature from Drexel University. His art has been exhibited at the Art Institute of Chicago, the Indianapolis Museum of Art, Cornell University, the University of Delaware, the Philadelphia Afro-American Historical and Cultural Museum, and the Schomburg Center for Black Culture in New York. He and his wife have four children and six grandchildren. They live in Croton-on-Hudson, New York.